Many years ago there [...]
one kingdom—Adamas [...] [...]
and rivalry caused the kingdom to be ripped in
two. The islands were ruled separately, as Aristo
and Calista, and the infamous Stefani coronation
diamond was split as a symbol of the feud, and
placed in the two new crowns.

But when the king divided the islands between his
son and daughter, he left them with these words:

*"You will rule each island for the good of the
people and bring out the best in your kingdom.
But my wish is that eventually these two jewels,
like the islands, will be reunited. Aristo and
Calista are more successful, more beautiful and
more powerful as one nation—Adamas."*

Now King Aegeus Karedes of Aristo is dead, and
the island's coronation diamond is missing! The
Aristans will stop at nothing to get it back, but
the ruthless sheikh king of Calista is hot on their
heels.

Whether by seduction, blackmail or marriage,
the jewel must be found. As the stories unfold,
secrets and sins from the past are revealed and
desire, love and passion war with royal duty. But
who will discover in time that it is innocence of
body and purity of heart that can unite the islands
of Adamas once again?

Read on for Carol Marinelli's insights into
THE ROYAL HOUSE OF KAREDES....

- **Did you enjoy writing The Royal House of Karedes?**
  I let my imagination fly. For the first few weeks I kept
  stalling over tiny details but, once I relaxed and let my
  characters be, the story flew.

- **What is your typical day?**
  I had a lightbulb moment recently—my sister told me
  that she leaves her house in the morning and comes
  back to it at night and it is exactly as she left it. That is
  normal! Now, I take the kids to school and then
  I come home and write. I also try to do nothing but
  be a mom between 3:00 p.m. and 9:00 p.m.

- **What did you like most about your characters?**
  I loved how awkward and shy Effie first appeared, yet
  just beneath the surface, she was intelligent and strong.
  And as the story revealed, there *was* something special
  about her—she just didn't know it yet. As for Zakari,
  he was my first sheikh, so he holds an extra-special
  place in my heart. I ♥ Zakari.

- **What would being part of a royal dynasty be like?**
  I can't think of a single thing that would make up
  for the lack of privacy. Though coffee and toast in bed
  each morning and gorgeous clothes might go some
  way to mollifying me!

- **Are diamonds really a girl's best friend?**
  No. Loving yourself is a girl's best friend (and then
  diamonds will follow—tee hee). Whether it's fake
  or real stones that adorn your fingers, happiness truly
  comes from within. However, if the right guy appeared
  bearing a ruby (and he'd taken the time to find out it
  was my favorite stone) I could, at a push, be won over...

Is the scarred sheikh the missing brother of King Zakari?
Don't miss the first book in the fabulous
Dark-Hearted Desert Men series,
Wedlocked: Banished Sheikh, Untouched Queen
by Carol Marinelli

Carol Marinelli

THE DESERT KING'S HOUSEKEEPER BRIDE

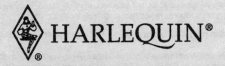

TORONTO • NEW YORK • LONDON
AMSTERDAM • PARIS • SYDNEY • HAMBURG
STOCKHOLM • ATHENS • TOKYO • MILAN • MADRID
PRAGUE • WARSAW • BUDAPEST • AUCKLAND

For Sam, Alex and Lucinda
Always
XXXX

ISBN-13: 978-0-373-12891-4

THE DESERT KING'S HOUSEKEEPER BRIDE

First North American Publication 2010.

Copyright © 2009 by Harlequin Books S.A.

Special thanks and acknowledgment are given to Carol Marinelli
for her contribution to *The Royal House of Karedes* series.

www.eHarlequin.com

Printed in U.S.A.

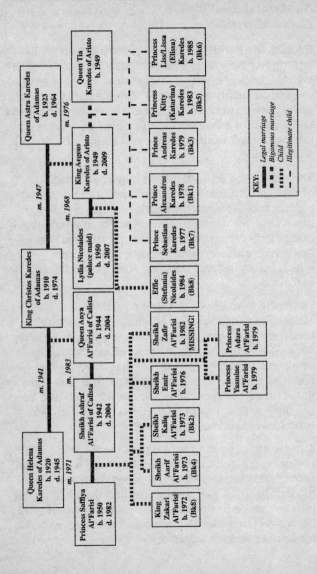

All about the author...
Carol Marinelli

CAROL MARINELLI finds writing a bio rather like writing her New Year's resolutions. Oh, she'd love to say that since she wrote the last one, she now goes to the gym regularly and doesn't stop for coffee and cake and a gossip afterward; that she's incredibly organized and writes for a few productive hours a day after tidying her immaculate house and taking a brisk walk with the dog.

The reality is, Carol spends an inordinate amount of time daydreaming about dark, brooding men and exotic places (research), which doesn't leave too much time for the gym, housework or anything that comes in between. And her most productive writing hours happen to be in the middle of the night, which leaves her in a constant state of bewildered exhaustion.

Originally from England, Carol now lives in Melbourne, Australia. She adores going back to the U.K. for a visit—actually, she adores going anywhere for a visit—and constantly (expensively) strives to overcome her fear of flying. She has three gorgeous children who are growing up so fast (too fast—they've just worked out that she lies about her age!) and keep her busy with a never-ending round of homework, sports and friends coming over.

A nurse and a writer, Carol writes for the Harlequin® Presents and Medical Romance lines and is passionate about both. She loves the fast-paced, busy setting of a modern hospital, but, every now and then admits it's bliss to escape to the glamorous, alluring world of her heroes and heroines in Harlequin Presents novels. A bit like her real life actually!

CHAPTER ONE

ONLY here could he find himself.

Staring out at the vast, shimmering emptiness, Sheikh King Zakari Al'Farisi of Calista welcomed the solitude of the Azahar desert. He ruled Calista and its people, but it was the desert that taught him how.

He was a good king—a strong ruler. Powerful, even ruthless at times—he did what had to be done. The easy path was never the option for Zakari and his people knew that and loved him for it. He stood six feet three and of solid build, his shoulders were wide enough to carry the hopes and fears of his land and his arms strong enough to hold any woman. He was considered a playboy at times, yet his people understood and forgave his one weakness, for no woman captured his mind for long—they were a mere temporary distraction that was necessary at times.

There was nothing temporary about the desert.

Zakari's eyes scanned the endless golden sea of sand, the landscape that shifted with the winds—while the rocks and canyons remained the solid markers.

It was the land that was the true master here—fierce, inhospitable, yet beautiful, always it humbled him, would drain and exhaust him and then replenish him. It was the test of the desert he needed now to remind him of his innate strength.

For many, times had changed their ways—four-wheel drives had replaced camels, shotguns were often used for prey instead of falconry, yet the desert and its vital principles were still ingrained and followed by some, and just as he watched out for them, fought to protect their simple existence, so too, while he was here, they would watch out for him. Sometimes in the distance, he would make out in the shimmer a small shadow, knew it was the nomadic tribesmen, keeping their caravan of camels far out of his sight as they travelled. Zakari knew they wouldn't invade his privacy, but was safe in the knowledge they were watching from a distance, making sure their king was safe and well when he returned to the land he loved.

He had asked, to his aides' horror, for solitude during the first part of his retreat here—no staff waiting on his every whim, nothing to distract him as he centred himself, as he focussed on finding the missing half of the Stefani diamond. And if he found it, *when* he found it, he would rule not just Calista, but Aristo too.

The legacy would be fulfilled.

King Christos Karedes had ruled both islands more than thirty years ago, yet the grumbles from his people had concerned him—the Aristan people worried they were not profiting enough from the diamond mines, the Calistan people eager to preserve their land and its gentle ways.

A wise king, Christos had known that the Aristans had to stop looking to Calista to support them. That they needed to build their own economy rather than rely on the Calistan diamonds. It was for that reason he decided to leave an island to each of his children and made the painful decision to split the precious Stefani diamond. His son and daughter would both become crowned rulers, with half the Stefani diamond in their new crowns.

Calista would be ruled by his daughter, Anya.

Aristo would be ruled by his son, Aegeus.

But time had moved on, shifting things like the sand in the desert.

Zakari's stepmother, Anya, had died five years ago along with his father—and now, with King Aegeus's sudden death, the islands were ripe for change.

Without the stone, the coronation of Aegeus's son Prince Alex could not go ahead and though the Aristan royals had tried to hide the fact the stone was missing, Zakari had, as he always did, found out.

Zakari sat, willing himself to concentrate, yet his mind, as it had these past couple of days, wandered. He was now quietly pleased at Hassan's suggestion that his housekeeper join him in his second week in the desert. When he returned to his tent at sunset, Christobel would be there. Would take care of him at night so that he could focus deeper by day as to how best to take care of the future of his people.

Zakari closed his eyes.

The people that he must protect from the lavish, insatiable ways of the neighbouring island, and protect too the diamond mines that the Aristans would love to get their greedy hands on.

And Zakari could get his revenge.

The wind swirled around him, the sand beat his face as the breeze picked up, but Zakari sat supremely still.

Soon, he would get his revenge on Aegeus for what he had done to Anya.

Haughty, razored features remained immobile as still he sat, then his full mouth softened in a ghost of a smile.

Revenge was so close he could taste it.

Craning her neck, Effie took a final lingering look at the palace as the helicopter lifted her into the late afternoon sky.

It was her first helicopter ride, and Effie knew she should be nervous, except she was too terrified at what lay ahead to worry about flying. The whole afternoon, in fact, had been like a wild roller-coaster ride.

It had started with whispers that Christobel—King Zakari's personal housekeeper—had, while the King was in the desert, run off with her latest boyfriend.

Christobel was always getting into trouble. In the two years Effie had been at the palace, it had always amazed her that Christobel *was* the King's personal housekeeper. When the staff had first heard that she'd run off, it had been more giggles and whispers, until the news had filtered through that Christobel was expected today to join the King on his retreat in the desert. A frantic search had ensued to find a suitable replacement, which had proved harder than usual. Two of the senior palace domestic staff were on leave, another was pregnant, another had children sick, until finally, to her absolute shock, Effie had been hastily considered for the position. With her mother dead and no other family to speak of, there was no reason she had to stay in Calista; the only blight had been her lack of experience with the actual royals. Effie was one of the lowliest palace maids, and her duties were usually reserved for tending to the more general areas of the palace.

'Nothing can be too much trouble for the King!' Stavroula said. 'For your time there you are on call day and night…'

'Of course!'

'The King has asked for no contact with the palace or his aides—he has demanded complete isolation. Christobel would have been the only one who would have assisted him with meals and housekeeping after his first week there. With all the troubles, he wants time alone right now.' Stavroula ran a worried hand over her brow. 'There is just *so* much trouble at the moment, Effie…'

There was.

Since King Aegeus's death, scandal abounded on the neighbouring island of Aristo, but Calista wasn't without its share of drama too. King Zakari's betrothed bride, Kalila, had, to everyone's shock, married the King's brother, Aarif, while their younger brother, Sheikh Kaliq, had recently married a lowly stable girl.

Oh, Stavroula was right, Effie knew that much— with so much unrest on both islands, there would be a lot for the King to think about.

'He demands complete solitude,' Stavroula explained. 'He has insisted there be no contact with the palace, so you cannot change your mind once you are there.'

'What if the King were taken ill?'

'He may well be.' Stavroula gave a worried shrug. 'But King Zakari, better than most, knows the test and demands of the desert… He feels it is what he needs right now—and what the King wants, the King gets…' Stavroula gave a pale smile—*compromise* wasn't exactly a word that equated with King Zakari. 'A helicopter is booked to bring you back next week. Until then it will be just you and the King.'

'I'll work hard.' Effie nodded eagerly.

'None of your chatter!' Stavroula sternly warned.

'He won't even know that I'm there,' Effie said earnestly.

Looking up at Effie's kind, plain, eager face, her dancing black curls and honest bright blue eyes, Stavroula relented a touch, because she knew that Effie would do everything possible for the King. 'These are turbulent times, Effie—we need our King to make wise choices. Our role seems meagre to many, but if the King is not troubled, if we can soothe his way, then he can come to the right decisions.

'Come now.' Clapping her hands, Stavroula stood up. 'There is no time to waste. Christobel was supposed to leave more than half an hour ago—the helicopter is waiting.'

'I need to pack.'

'There isn't time,' Stavroula said, hurrying Effie through the palace and dragging Christobel's pale blue suitcase behind her. 'You'll just have to make do with Christobel's things.'

Which would be fine, Effie thought, except Christobel was about half her size, but Stavroula brushed off her protests. 'The wind is picking up.' They were dashing across the manicured lawns of the palace to the waiting chopper. 'If the helicopter doesn't leave now, there might not be another chance till tomorrow. The King cannot be kept waiting!'

The green lawns alone were a testament to Zakari's wealth as the palace was built on the edge of the desert.

The rear rooms had sweeping views, and Effie had often found herself gazing out to the desert as she worked, but seeing it from above, watching the palace fade into the distance, it wasn't just nerves that danced in her stomach, but a flicker of excitement too.

Of all the royals that she had glimpsed, of all the princes and cousins and sheikhs that peppered her meagre existence, it had always been Zakari who had enthralled her the most.

She occasionally glimpsed him throughout her working day in the palace, his clothing as chameleon as his complex character. Whether he was striding to a function in military finery, or sweeping through the palace in traditional robes, always he looked spectacular, but never more so, for Effie, than when in Western clothes.

More glamorous and as effortlessly fashionable as any of the Aristans, to Effie he looked like a film star, but the real treat had been when first she'd seen him smile. Oh, not at her, but one morning, when she'd been dashing through the corridors, carrying sheets, frantically trying to get the endless spare bedrooms prepared for a looming royal wedding, she'd flattened herself against a wall as the King had strode past, chatting and talking with his brother, the soon-to-be married Kaliq. Kaliq, a dashing playboy himself, must have said something funny to the King, because suddenly Zakari's haughty face had broken into a wide smile, his full mouth parting, and for Effie it had been like watching the sunrise. Effie had felt trapped by its rare, majestic beauty, so much so that she had even forgotten to duck and curtsy and had actually forgotten to lower her head and avert her eyes.

Not that he'd noticed.

Not that Zakari would ever notice her.

But in that second alone Effie had understood how he had earned every flicker of his heartbreak reputation.

With just one smile, he'd captured her heart.

And now she was going to be alone with him.

Being stranded in the desert with a moody, demanding boss might not be many people's idea of a good time, but Effie took her job seriously—and here was a chance to prove herself. To work hard for the king she adored and, as Stavroula had pointed out, in her own meagre way, help the people of Calista during these turbulent times.

As the chopper landed the pilot threw out her case, anxious to leave before the winds picked up further, he explained, and Effie quickly jumped down.

The heat was stifling.

The dry air was so hot that it actually hurt as she dragged it into her lungs. The flimsy scarf she held over her mouth and nose did nothing to protect her eyes, though, and Effie ducked her head, but running under the whirring rotors was too much in the heat and even that short burst of exertion exhausted her. The sand was whirring around, gravelling in her ears, eyes and her hair as the chopper lifted, but even when it was gone the shifting sands didn't settle. With the sand pummelling her legs and face Effie stood for a moment, witnessing first-hand the endless landscape, broken only by the vast orange canyons that the wind whistled through. Only then did it truly dawn on Effie just how isolated they were. Having grown up in the poorer part of Calista, and having spent much of her time nursing her ailing mother, Effie was no stranger to hardship or roughing it and hard work certainly didn't faze her, yet a flutter of angst for the unknown swirled inside her as

Effie saw King Zakari's huge tent, still but a speck in the vast scheme of the desert.

She didn't expect him to come out and greet her— why would a king greet a housekeeper? And she had been told that he would disappear early in the mornings and not return until after sunset, which was still a couple of hours away.

She would start work straight away, Effie decided, quelling her nerves by forming a plan. By the time King Zakari returned, she'd have familiarised herself with things, and would be fully in control of everything that he might request from her. Quickly realising the wheels didn't work in the sand, she lifted Christobel's heavy case, damp circles forming under her arms, her face no doubt red from the heat and exertion as she walked the final distance. Effie made a quick addition to her list—she would have a long cool drink, *then* she would start work!

The tent was cool and dark as she parted the fabric, stepped inside and removed her shoes. Her eyes took a moment to adjust from the brightness outside, the howl of the wind subdued now as she slowly wandered into the blissful retreat. Rugs were thickly scattered on the floor and were plump and soft beneath her bare feet. They lined the walls of the tent too, making the large area more intimate. The space was broken with low, ornate tables surrounded by thick runs of cushioned fabric, and an entire wall was hung with drapes while the floor was scattered with jewel-coloured cushions of velvet and satin, which were so plump Effie would have loved to sink into them.

It *was* a mess though!

Sand had been trailed through the abode, and tiny jewelled cups and plates, along with jugs, littered the surfaces.

Effie left her case and set about exploring further, finding the kitchen area, marvelling that even in the middle of the desert the King's wealth meant she could gulp icy water from the dispenser on the fridge and could run her hand in cool water and splash her face.

She stared at the sumptuous foods in the massive fridges and pantries—if the helicopter didn't return for a year, they wouldn't starve! And here, behind the kitchen area, was clearly the staff quarters—small curtained-off areas, which contained simple mattresses and furnishings, but still with all mod cons. Effie realised, awash with relief, that she was actually looking forward to her time in the desert. With King Zakari out from sunrise to sunset, and nothing but a tent, no matter how vast, to take care of, it was going to be a holiday compared to her work in the palace!

Smiling to herself, Effie gathered her tools—first she would sweep out his room and make his bed.

No man, no prince, and certainly no king made their own.

She would change the sheets, then draw him a long bath.

When King Zakari returned from his wandering, he wouldn't mind a scrap that his regular housekeeper hadn't been able to come. He'd soon see she could work harder and *better* than Christobel.

Zakari was growing impatient; he knew that she was here, so why didn't she just come to him?

Mindful of the gathering wind, he had returned early from the desert and had bathed slowly—appreciative of the luxury his title afforded. That was what the desert did, he reflected, the water coursing down his toned body as he stood up, the rich oils making it bead on his olive skin. It made him appreciate the essentials in life that he usually took for granted.

And sex to Zakari was *essential.*

He didn't smoke, or drink, his body was in superb condition and, despite his love of horses and his passion for polo, on unique principle he refused to gamble any of the vast fortune his title afforded him. He would win by more calculated means.

Women were his only weakness.

And a very safe bet they were too, Zakari thought with just a glimmer of discontentment—the cards he held in his royal hand meant he always, without fail, won.

Only one woman hadn't fallen for his charms.

Princess Kalila Zadar had long been deemed a suitable bride by his father—a woman who had been betrothed to him since she was little more than a child.

And though he far from relished the prospect of marrying, Zakari had realised his people wanted to see their king settled, that at thirty-seven years of age it was time to start producing heirs. Reluctantly he had bowed to pressure, instructing his chief aide, Hassan, to set the wheels for the long-awaited royal wedding in motion and, because he was busy trying to find the missing Stefani diamond he had sent his brother, Sheikh Aarif, to Hadiya to collect his promised bride.

Aarif and Kalila had fallen in love…

Terrified of his wrath, they had tried to deny it, yet Aarif had confessed, stunned at Zakari's reaction.

Zakari had been overjoyed at the news and had been genuinely pleased to see his brother for once happy, just privately bemused as to why.

Oh, Kalila would have made a perfect king's wife,

but there had not been a flicker of want when finally he had met her, not a flicker of what might have been as she wed his brother. Just genuine joy for his brother's happiness and the hollow realisation that not once had he ever come close to experiencing those feelings Kalila and Aarif had for each other.

He was a king, Zakari reminded himself.

Kings did not have time for romance.

He did not shave—his strong jaw had several days' growth. Zakari never shaved when he was on retreat, and, anyway, there was no need to impress Christobel.

His title took care of that.

Soon... He could feel the fire in his groin that made him mortal.

Tonight he could just be a man.

Tomorrow he would return to the desert and carry on being King.

Hearing the chopper, Zakari had picked up a towel and wandered through his desert abode. He had dried his chest as he walked, naked, utterly at ease in his own skin. He had pulled back the drape, he had watched the helicopter land, the temporary sandstorm blurring his vision, but he had seen Christobel's pale blue suitcase and instantly he had been hard at the prospect of what imminently lay ahead.

Closing the drape, he had then headed back to his opulent sleeping area—a king did not rush out to greet anyone.

She would greet him.

Wandering back, he had considered dressing for about half a second—but why?

It had been a week without release and, now that it was close, suddenly his need was urgent.

His bed was scattered with cushions, and he half sat, half lay on the bed, waiting for her. Christobel would not distract his mind with senseless chatter, or demand a tender reunion—she knew why she was here.

Closing his eyes, he smiled to himself…

Just as she would smile when she walked in and saw him lying there…

Imagining her skilled lips around his length and the sweet release they would quickly bring, he gripped his magnificent member, stroking it to its full impressive length. He could hear the pad of her walking, the swish of drapes as she drew nearer, and he continued to stroke himself slowly, waiting for her soft gasp of approval, knowing that no words would be uttered as Christobel entered…her duties were as urgent as they were apparent…

Effie had thought he was out—the silence, along with Stavroula's instructions, had indicated he would be in the desert now. As she had walked to his sleeping quarters, her only thought had been the beauty of her surrounds, that here in the desert had been created an abode as stunning in its own right as the palace, but walking into the room she had frozen.

He was beautiful.

It had been her first thought as his raw, naked form had greeted her.

Even the opulent jewel-coloured bed, with its feast of cushions and silks, looked shabby in comparison to his gleaming beauty.

His muscles rippled beneath silky olive skin, his jet hair was wet from bathing. His eyes were closed, his lashes forming shadows that cast down to razored cheekbones as Effie's own eyes too slowly wandered down.

Wide shouldered, his arms were long yet muscular, his chest smooth, his stomach taut and flat, with an ebony trail that snaked from his umbilicus. One muscular leg was flat on the bed, his knee raised up on the other leg, and then her eyes saw what she never should have.

Oh, a dresser might hold a towel, might avert her eyes.

But she had never been of that status.

And surely a dresser wouldn't expect to see this.

But in that split second, before her eyes shuttered, she saw long, slender fingers, loosely holding his vast member. He was stroking the taut rigidity in slow sensual strokes that had Effie standing rigid, and for an appalling, shame-filled second she watched with morbid fascination, because quite simply it was the most beautiful, most erotic thing she had ever seen. She knew she should silently leave, should make a discreet exit, and that was what she attempted, but her own body didn't seem to be working any more. The broom she had been holding so tightly dropped to the floor with a heavy thud as Effie let out a horrified breath.

'I'm sorry…' Covering her eyes as his snapped open, she tried to back off, tried to turn around, but her legs were like jelly. 'Your Majesty, I am so very sorry…'

He was off the bed in a trice, but her hand over her eyes wasn't going to stop her from hearing his rapid curse, nor the terrifying feel of him thundering across the room towards her.

'Where's Christobel?'

'She couldn't come, Your Highness…'

She was tempted to fall to her knees to beg forgiveness, but to be on eye level with *that*… All she could do was stand with her eyes covered and say over and over that she was sorry, so very, very sorry!

'I should have called out—it was my fault for creeping up…' She could hardly breathe, the desert heat nothing compared to her flaming face and she was drenched in sweat, just appalled. 'I will go…' she pleaded, her legs moving now. 'You just carry on…' She wanted to be calm, only she wasn't, wanted to take away his embarrassment a touch… They would be here for days, after all.

'Carry on?' he demanded. 'Carry on what?'

'Pleasuring yourself.' Effie cringed, then attempted a more sophisticated air; actually peeled off her hand from her eyes, relief drenching her as she saw he was at least now covered with one of the bed throws. 'As you have every right to. I'll go now!'

She turned, walked quickly, just desperate to get out of there, stunned when a hand grabbed her wrist, when Sheikh King Zakari Al'Farisi spun her around to face him—fury in his inky black eyes.

'You think I was pleasuring myself?' he shouted. 'I am Sheikh King Zakari Al'Farisi—I do not have to pleasure myself.'

'But…' Effie frowned, stunned at his rage, as if only *now* was he embarrassed, only *now* was he aggrieved, her eyes widening in horror and realisation. When next he spoke that wide mouth she had once seen parted in pleasure was now twisted in contempt.

'You,' he roared, 'were the one sent to pleasure me!"

CHAPTER TWO

SHE could never go out there again.

Never!

Face-down on her bed, writhing with humiliation, sobbing in utter shame and fear, Effie considered her options.

Wander out now into the desert and disappear for ever?

Or put on a smile and make dinner?

The desert seemed the gentler option.

How could she possibly face him now? Yet how could she not?

Was that what Stavroula had meant by on call day and night?

Nothing was too much trouble for the King?

And he was furious with her too! Her rabid apologies had only made things worse!

Her job was over, except she couldn't even leave... Effie wept at the hopelessness of it all—even her womb was weeping in sympathy, proving the impossibility of her plight. For even if she were of that sort, even if she did know how to pleasure not just a man, but the King, it was her monthly time and she couldn't.

And she was stuck here for days!

'Here!'

For the second time in an hour she froze.

Face-down in the pillow, she froze at the deep sound of his voice, felt his imposing presence in the room. Only this time it was without anger, his voice utterly calm and even when next he spoke.

'I have made you a drink… Take it…'

The King had made her a drink!

Stunned, she turned over and looked at the tiny jewelled cup he offered. She took it, lifting the cup to her lips and tasting the thick sweet syrupy coffee, taking comfort from its warmth. Though the sugary drink wasn't exactly helping her to recover from her shock. If anything she was more stunned than ever that Sheikh King Zakari was not just in her room, but actually talking to her without anger, her confusion increasing when finally she dared to look and saw that there was almost a smile on his face.

'Can I know your name?'

"Effie.' She struggled to get up, to remember her place. 'Your Highness, I cannot tell you how sorr—'

'Enough!' He halted her stammering repeat of an apology with one word and after a moment's consideration he actually sat down on the bed beside her and just stared at her for the longest time.

For an hour Zakari had heard her weeping.

As he had dressed, his initial anger had faded into wry amusement. Zakari didn't do embarrassment—a flash of anger perhaps, for what she had thought she had found, but embarrassment—no.

He had heard her embarrassment, though.

And, once his anger *and* disappointment that Christobel had failed to arrive had faded, he had realised what had happened—and had also realised her fear.

And, given they had several days still to spend isolated in the desert, he had chosen, as he often did, to address the latest problem to arrive in his life directly.

'I thought you were Christobel—she was due to arrive this afternoon and naturally when I saw her case come out of the helicopter...'

'She left the palace this morning, Your Highness.' Effie's teeth were chattering; she was terrified of speaking directly with the King, yet she was grateful for the chance to explain herself. 'I was chosen as a replacement at the last minute. There was no time for me to pack—I have to wear her things...'

Zakari glanced at her generous flesh, but didn't comment.

'I thought you were in the desert, that you wouldn't return till sunset. I wanted to prepare your room for you.' Effie gave a helpless shrug. 'Stavroula did say that I am to be on call day and night, that nothing was to be too much trouble for you. She tried to make it clear to me what my duties would be and I was so eager in my acceptance, I truly didn't understand... I don't know about these things.'

'Stavroula meant cleaning, preparing my meals—if I require a drink or conversation perhaps...' Zakari explained. 'What happened this afternoon—' he dismissed the entire event with one flick of a manicured hand '—Christobel and I had our own private arrangement...'

'Oh...' Effie frowned, realising only now *why* the irresponsible, rather lazy Christobel held such an esteemed position!

'So I'm not here for... I mean, you don't expect me to...'

'No.' Zakari withered at the very thought, though he

didn't show it. He was used to reed-thin, groomed and skilled lovers—the thought of this plain, plump, blushing woman taking Christobel's place made his response quite definite!

'And you *do* need a housekeeper?'

He neither wanted nor needed a housekeeper, but as he stared down at her tear-streaked face something unfamiliar twisted inside him, the same twist that had responded to her cries, and the same twist that had sent a king to make a maid a drink.

'Yes…' He frowned at his own response—confused that he was actually placating her, when always, *always* it was the other way around. 'I do need a housekeeper, but not tonight. Unpack your things and then rest. You will commence your duties tomorrow.'

He swept out then—leaving Effie blinking on the bed, reeling at the turn of events.

The shame, the appallingness of what had taken place, dimmed by sheer bemusement.

The King had made her a drink and had consoled her in her shame.

King Zakari had made the impossible suddenly better.

On shaky legs she stood, unclipping the suitcase as he had instructed, and pulled back the lid, her hands shaking, her face darkening red as she went through the contents. Her head was tight with sinful curiosity as Christobel and the King's *private arrangement* revealed itself further.

Apart from one token maid's outfit that would be way too tight on Effie, it was silk stockings that slid through her fingers, silver-foil-wrapped condoms that glistened in the make-up bag, suspender belts and sheer bras that wouldn't cover a pimple, that over and over mocked

Effie's innocence. Lotions and potions that Christobel must use to weave her magic had Effie wide-eyed with shock, and, pulling out a flimsy robe and the spare uniform that were the only remotely decent objects, she quickly slammed the case closed and tried to forget what she'd seen. She'd wear the same clothes all week rather than touch Christobel's stuff! Having washed out her own underwear and dress to wear in the morning, Effie slipped between the cool sheets. The flimsy robe and uniform lay draped over the chair, should Zakari call her, and Effie willed herself to relax, only she couldn't. She turned off the small bedside lamp and willed the rest Zakari too had instructed to come to her, but for the first time she defied the King's orders.

Switching the lamp back on, she retrieved the case. Her eyes narrowed in curiosity this time as slowly she went through the contents, rubbing lipsticks on the backs of her hands, spraying perfume in the air, then, removing the lid on one of the containers, Effie inhaled the sickly sweet smell of depilatory cream. Oh, she might be naive but she wasn't stupid. Effie knew there were no fancy waxing clinics in Calista as there were on Aristo, that for Christobel to be groomed, she would have to take care of that herself.

Staring down at her own body, Effie could see the coarse hair on her legs, the thick curls that hid her womanhood, and for the first time she cared—cared that they were there. Wishing her body were smooth and soft and beautiful enough… Then cursed herself for even daring to think such things. Ramming the lid back on the container, she angrily turned off the light, refusing to think about it, except her mind wouldn't listen, wouldn't give her the quiet she craved.

She had entered a different world today, seen things she'd never thought she would. Effie screwed her eyes tightly closed and willed sleep to come, only it wasn't the King or the desert that worried her... Her wildest dreams were a pale version to today's events.

Here in the desert Zakari liked to prepare his own simple breakfast—

But this morning he was greeted with a feast.

He returned to the aroma of fresh fatir, a sweet pancake pastry Effie had prepared. Tiny bowls with ground almonds in argan oil and honey waited on the table for him, along with cheeses, sweet syrupy fruits and the usual strong, sweet treacle of coffee, but she had also made a refreshing mint tea.

'This is good,' Zakari said with unexpected enthusiasm as he took a bite of the fatir. He had the best chefs, was used only to excellent food being served to him, yet fatir, properly prepared, well, there was little better.

'It's my mother's recipe.' Effie smiled.

'She is a good cook!'

'She was.' He watched her smile falter. 'She died two years ago. She was once a palace maid at Aristo. She used to make it—'

'They would not have fatir there,' Zakari interrupted with a sneer. 'There it is all French pastries, and croissants. At least here on Calista we have tradition still!'

'I'm sure you're right,' Effie duly agreed, 'but my mother worked there many years ago, before I was born.'

'When King Christos was alive.' Zakari smiled at the memory of a man he had never met, then graciously conceded the point to Effie. 'They would have had fatir in the palace then. And argan…' He dipped the pastry in the rare oil, and offered it to her. Shocked, Effie refused.

'Sit,' Zakari ordered. 'For days I have spoken to no one. As a housekeeper here in the desert you can speak with me when I choose.' He held out the pastry dripping with oil and she took it. 'However,' Zakari reminded, 'when we return to the palace I will ignore you.'

'Of course!' Effie demurred, stunned when he smiled, and lost, just lost, by the effect of that coveted smile when aimed at her.

'That was a joke,' Zakari said. 'If I see you, of course, I will greet you. So how is the argan?' he asked, as Effie glowed at the thought of the King acknowledging her back at the palace!

'It's wonderful.' She had eaten fatir before, but hers was always sweetened just with honey. The argan oil was a luxury, liquid gold, produced from trees that grew only in Southwest Morocco. It was a delicacy and it tasted divine.

'It is good for energy,' Zakari explained. 'It is also considered…' he hesitated when he saw a dull flush spread on her cheeks, realising that after yesterday's goings-on an aphrodisiac perhaps wasn't required at breakfast this morning '…to have many medicinal benefits,' he offered instead, and as Effie watched that handsome, unscrupulous face again soften with a smile it was easy for her to smile too. 'My mother too always insisted on fatir.'

'Your real mother or Queen Anya?'

It was an innocent question, the easiness of their chatter, the informality he had engineered all serving to knock her off guard, but seeing his eyes narrow, the sudden rigidity of his features, Effie could have bitten off her tongue, inwardly cursing herself for forgetting Stavroula's stern warning, because once again she was in trouble.

'Your job is to listen!' Zakari snapped. 'Not to question.'

'Of course, Your Highness…' Effie stood, cheeks flaming, busying herself with clearing dishes away, rueing that she had mentioned a subject that was clearly out of bounds. But as she turned for the staff area Zakari's words halted her.

'My first mother.' His voice was softer now, his eyes kinder, when finally Effie turned around. 'My first mother insisted we eat fatir in the morning.'

Scared of saying the wrong thing again, Effie nodded.

'I have enjoyed my breakfast this morning. Tomorrow, though,' Zakari said, 'I just want coffee. I like to live simply during my time here.'

'You can't go out to the desert without eating!' Effie snapped her mouth closed, terrified she'd gone too far again, only breathing again when instead of scolding her he took another bite of the fatir she had so skilfully made and again compromised. 'Coffee and fatir…' he relented. 'But that is to be all.'

The winds of yesterday had wreaked change.

As Zakari set off into the desert he surveyed the endlessly shifting landscape.

If lost, the rocks—the constants—would guide him, were guiding him now, Zakari reminded himself, even if he felt abandoned. His search for the missing half of the diamond had taken many twists and turns. Since

Aegeus's death, when he had discovered that the stone had been replaced with a fake, his search had been relentless, taking him to Egypt, to America and to London. Some small Aristan pieces of jewellery had turned up at the most exclusive of auctions, and Zakari had purchased them back anonymously, positive now that Aegeus had kept a lover whom he had showered with gifts—and, Zakari concluded, perhaps even the stone.

But who?

Every lead he had followed seemed to take him further from the truth, every jewel that turned up confused the picture more. There had been rumours she had been a maid, but that search had proved fruitless; rumours too of a mistress during the early years of Aegeus's marriage, but if there had been, then Aegeus had been more than discreet.

At every turn, there was nothing

That was why he was here, why he had chosen to retreat to the desert. The craziness of the past few months, Aegeus's death, his son Sebastian relinquishing his right to the throne, his own brothers' weddings, his pursuit of the stone... Zakari had chosen to clear his head, to come to the rich land and humbly ask for its help.

He wandered, only aimlessly now.

Effie speaking of his mother, *daring* to speak of his mother, had kindled something... First a flicker of a memory of a time when life was uncomplicated, running through their palace, in another land, another time, the sound of laughter from his mother.

His real mother.

He had not been born to be King of Calista and for

a while that had troubled his mind and no doubt the people of Calista too.

His mother had died while giving birth to her seventh child, Zafir. His father, Sheikh Ashraf Al'Farisi, the third son of the ruling family of the Sheikhdom of Hadiya, had, after a period of grieving, fallen in love with Queen Anya, the ruler of Calista.

Unable to have children herself, she had raised and loved Ashraf's children as her own, and had groomed Zakari to one day be King. A day that still should not have happened, that should still be in the distance, except Ashraf and Anya had been killed in a helicopter crash and the weight of the grieving island had fallen onto his shoulders.

Now, five years on, and at thirty-seven years of age, he felt the weight of responsibility had never been greater, or so willingly carried.

Power was everything to Zakari.

Finding the jewel his sole mission now.

So why, Zakari demanded of himself, couldn't he concentrate on doing just that?

The day was long. Zakari had disappeared after breakfast and Effie had set about cleaning, happy to be busy so that she didn't have to think about the events of yesterday!

There was a lot to be done.

He might make his own food and drinks but he didn't wash a plate or cup. Clothes and towels littered the carpeted floors, and Effie set about picking up and washing and cleaning, indulging in a teeny fantasy of doing *such* a good job, of being *so* unobtrusive, yet so breathtakingly efficient, that Zakari might, on return to the palace, select her to replace Christobel as his personal housekeeper—for housekeeping duties only, though, Effie amended, her face suddenly on fire!

Only late in the day did she summon the nerve to prepare his sleeping area, her blush returning as she entered his room.

She set about sweeping the floor and dusting the dark ornate furniture, before finally pulling the endless pillows and cushions from his vast bed and changing the silk sheets. No matter how she tried not to think about it—in fact, the more she tried *not* to think about it—over and over she did. She just couldn't banish *that* image of King Zakari from her mind.

Effie knew her place and, unlike many, there wasn't a resentful bone in her body. Her mother had raised her to adore the royals. They had been generous to her, Lydia had explained. Her hard work at the palace when she was younger had been rewarded by a generous package when she had left, and with wise investment it had meant they had a home and a moderate income despite Lydia never working.

Effie had never questioned it.

Just as she didn't question why some should have everything, while others had nothing. She felt privileged to work in the palace. Even if she only got to clean the fineries, still she could gaze upon them. Even if she only polished the silver and jewels, still she got to hold them in her hands.

It could never be hers.

She accepted that.

Just as the man she had glimpsed in naked, sensual beauty could never, would never, lavish his attention on her.

Yet there was this unfamiliar thrill in the pit of her stomach as she recalled what she had witnessed. She bit on her lip as she dragged off the sheet. The flurry of the silk had his masculine scent lingering in the air, and, just for a moment, for a tiny daring, fleeting moment...Effie wished.

For the first time ever, she wished it could be that the treasure she had surveyed might be hers for even a little while. Burying her face in the sheets he had graced, she inhaled him to her very soul.

Wished she were as slim and as beautiful as Christobel.

Wished the King had been waiting for her.

Wished she didn't disappoint.

Still, she wasn't being paid to dream, so Effie got on with her work, and over the next couple of days an easy routine developed between them.

Zakari rose at sunrise as Effie prepared breakfast. He usually ate in silence in the morning. Occasionally he might ask if she'd slept well, or murmur a brief thank you, but generally he was sullen, pensive and silent. In fact, for Effie it was almost a relief, really, when he wandered off to the desert, to return after sunset.

Only it was a different Zakari that returned.

He would bathe and change, then eat the meal she had prepared alone. Afterwards, when he sat on the low cushions and drank his coffee as Effie cleared away his meal, he would start talking to her.

Mindful of Stavroula's harsh warning and the mistakes she had already made, Effie tried to hold on to her tongue, but Sheikh King Zakari Al'Farisi was such engaging company in the evenings that it was all too easy to unbend, to talk about her family, to chatter and linger for a little while longer. Her reward—that unscrupulous face broke into his heart-stopping smile when she offered a silly joke, and, most surprisingly of all, he didn't silence her when occasionally she bantered with him.

Sheikh King Zakari despised the Aristan royals, yet Effie adored them, and refused to bend to his thinking.

'The Aristan royals looked after my mother well,' Effie said stoutly one night as she stacked some plates. 'I'm saving up my money to go to Aristo for Prince Alex's coronation in January.'

There would be no coronation for Prince Alex in January if he found the jewel, Zakari thought darkly. Not that Effie would know about such things. The only thing the two royal families did agree on was that the fact the jewel was missing must remain a fiercely guarded secret.

'You really think that Alex will make a good king?' Zakari poured scorn on her words. 'His brother Sebastian was the one raised to be king, yet he denounced the throne to marry a woman who wasn't suitable.'

'But that's lovely,' Effie insisted.

'That is weak!' Zakari dismissed her sentiment. 'The people of Aristo are worried by this behaviour. They know that Alex and his new wife do not really want to take the role and all that it will entail.'

'Well, I'm not worried.'

'You live in Calista,' Zakari pointed out, 'so you have no need to be. Their turmoil does not affect you— you have a strong king.'

'I do!' Effie flushed. 'I have a wonderful king, who I am proud to serve, but I still care about Aristo and I think, under Queen Tia's guidance, that Prince Alex will make a wonderful king!'

Effie remained adamant, and Zakari could only admire her loyalty as instead of backing down she gave him a brief smile, and wished him goodnight before heading out to the staff area.

She had made a good point too, Zakari reflected, lying back on the cushions and closing his eyes for a moment. His body was exhausted from his long day, but his mind was still alert. Queen Tia was, as far as he was concerned, Aristo's only saving grace. An elegant, dignified woman, she had stood loyal and demure by Aegeus's side and had poured herself into her children and charities and had, Zakari reluctantly admitted, raised her children well. Zakari had always admired Prince Sebastian, at least until he had turned his back on his people for a woman.

Effie *was* interesting to talk to, though, and with the night stretching ahead of him Zakari considered calling her back. He actually missed her when she retired, missed those sparkling, lively blue eyes, and the way she blushed just a little when she laughed, but he stopped himself. Maybe it was cabin fever that was causing it, but Zakari was starting to realise that he spoke too much when she was around. Under her steady gaze, it was all too easy to forget the rules, to forget the discretion, the distance that was usually carved into every shred of his DNA.

So, instead of calling her, he retired too, not to his luxurious bed, but outside, preparing a fire, then stretching out beneath the stars and listening to the call of the desert, remembering Effie's place, because he could never, ever forget his.

Yet on the sixth night, as he sat on the low cushions and the table was cleared and there was no reason for her to remain, he asked her to join him.

'You do not live in the palace?'

'I have a small cottage.' Effie nodded, colour roaring up her cheeks as she tentatively took a seat on the cushion beside him. 'Well, it was my mother's.'

'You said she was a palace maid, though—how could she afford it?'

'She was a maid before I was born,' Effie said, 'but she saved her money well and invested it wisely. It's only a tiny cottage, but with her savings, well, they lasted almost till she died. She never had to work again.'

She was so naïve. Zakari smothered a smile. The only single mothers who owned real estate in Calista worked *extremely* hard for their money! Still, it was sweet, Zakari reflected, that she genuinely didn't seem to know that she believed the lies her mother must have fed her.

'You miss her a lot?'

'Terribly.' He saw a sparkle of tears in her eyes that she rapidly blinked back. 'You must miss your mother too,' Effie said. 'Or, rather, mothers.' He didn't scold her this time, just gave a curt nod at her observation. Losing his mother at the age of eleven had been hard, but losing Anya five years ago had been just as bad. Zakari had never been particularly close to his father; they had respected each other, but there had never been any real conversation, let alone affection. With Anya it had been different. She had doted on him as if he were her own flesh and blood, had helped him navigate the terrifying prospect that one day he would be ruler and King, as well as confiding in him as to her own fears and pain. Zakari was only half listening as Effie chatted on, but he frowned her to silence when next she spoke. '…and with what happened to your youngest brother too…'

'That is not for discussion.' This time Zakari did

speak sternly. He wanted to hear about her, not to discuss how he might feel about things. 'So, it is nice that you have your own home…' But she wasn't so receptive now. No matter how he tried to cajole her to freely talk, the easiness between them had gone as Effie answered with only the minimum of responses.

Naive and sweet she might be, Zakari thought, but there was much more to her than just that. There was this intelligence in her eyes, this stubbornness within her, that over the days had entranced him—and never more so than now. Though she remained eternally polite, still she wouldn't relent, refused to play the court jester just to amuse him. What was more, Zakari realised, after yet another monotone answer, Effie wouldn't reveal anything more of herself if he did not grace her with the same.

Without a word she demanded from him something he rarely bestowed.

Real conversation.

'You would make an excellent chess player…' The edge of his mouth lifted into a smile at another monotone, polite answer as she forced him to ponder his next move. Zakari wondered whether opening up would box him in, or somehow release him.

'I doubt it.' Effie smiled softly. 'I don't play games.'

After the longest hesitation, weighing up her kind, sympathetic face through narrow, mistrusting eyes, Zakari chose the latter.

'Every day I think of him.' It was Zakari who broke the endless strained silence. He had never admitted such things—even to himself—could hear the unchecked words coming from his usually guarded lips, only he did nothing to halt them. 'Still now, in my heart of hearts, I cannot accept that he is dead.'

'So you cannot grieve…' Hearing his pain on instinct, she touched him, her hand reaching for his forearm, but the moment contact was made she realised the inappropriateness, pulled her hand back and bunched it into a fist, yet she could feel the tingle in her fingers.

Zakari, in turn, was struggling. He had let her glimpse his pain, had shared enough that surely now she should continue, now she should talk, so that he might relax. Yet that brush on his arm, that mere hint of contact, had brought rare comfort. His black eyes pondered hers, acknowledging that lonely raw piece of his soul had, for just a fleeting second perhaps, been understood.

He *had* never grieved.

Had never been *allowed* to grieve.

A prince who would one day be king could not cry.

Anya had grieved. For a second his mind flashed back to Anya, sobbing on the bed. How he had wanted to weep with her, yet he had been sixteen—a king in training. As he stared at Effie, her sapphire eyes pooling with tears, his left shoulder tightened and he could feel again his father's hand placed *there*.

'Stay strong!' His father, Sheikh Ashraf, had squeezed his son's shoulder, when Zakari had wanted to be held. 'It is not for us to demand answers.'

He had never questioned it, yet under her gentle presence he questioned it now.

'Can I ask what happened?'

Her voice was as soft as his growling response. 'You know what happened.'

'I know what I read,' Effie countered, 'I know what I heard, but I don't *know*.'

'You know what you need to.'

'It might help to talk.'

'How?' he asked, and Effie realised he truly didn't know. Here before her was a man whose feelings had never come into things—who had been raised to act, rather than to feel.

'It just might.' She could have wept; not for his brother, but for the flicker of confusion in those guarded eyes. She could almost feel him relent and then recoil with every second that passed. What came so easily to her was unfathomable to him.

And then he gave her the sweetest gift of all. Sheikh King Zakari Al'Farisi, with painful words, invited her into his world and, Effie realised, she would love him for ever for it.

'Emir, my brother, was sick, he had the flu…' His strong voice was reduced to a hoarse whisper as he continued. 'I never played with the younger children. I was raised to be king—it was not my place to do childish things…

'Aarif and Kaliq, the twins, were creeping off to build a raft… They were teenage boys, they should have known better, but they were silly, planning this adventure that they would build a raft and sail out on it to sea. Zafir found out about their plans…' His voice caught for a moment, but she calmly sat, just waited till he was ready to continue. 'He begged to go with them. They lost control; they were swept to sea…'

She had heard bits about the tragedy that had happened when Effie was just four years old. She had seen for herself the scar on Prince Aarif's face where he had been shot, and had read bits about it in the library, but hearing it from the King himself, from the brother who had lost so much, had the tears spilling from Effie's eyes.

'They were captured by diamond smugglers. Zafir was a proud little thing—he shouted to them who his father was. Of course, as soon as the smugglers realised just who it was they had captured they became greedy. They bound their wrists with ropes; Aarif and Kaliq still have the scars of the ropes that cut in as the smugglers debated the ransom they would demand…

'On Calista, the palace was frantic. I remember the search going out, the helicopters and boats…' Zakari shook his head. 'It was Zafir that got free, he untied his elder brothers and they ran to the raft and set off. They almost got away, but they were spotted. Aarif was shot in the face; you can see the scars he bears…'

Effie nodded solemnly.

'They are nothing to his pain inside.

'Aarif fell into the sea; of course Kaliq jumped in to save his twin—they tried to get to the raft, but the sea pulled it away, with Zafir still on it. The smugglers recaptured the twins, beat them again and again…my father paid the ransom for his two sons…but Zafir…' He couldn't continue, so Effie did it for him.

'He has never been heard of since.'

'Had he lived, he would be turning twenty-seven this very week. Zafir would be a man.'

'Maybe he is alive…' Effie offered, but Zakari closed his eyes and shook his head. 'My heart says that he is, my head tells me he is dead, that I must now let him rest, yet at my very core I cannot.' He shook his head now— never had he revealed so much and it had utterly depleted him. Her comfort, the empathy in her eyes, seemed to be invading him now. 'I will retire now.'

Without another word he did just that, leaving Effie sitting blinking for a moment, before forcing herself to stand, to plump up the cushions and tidy the area ready for the morning. She laid the table for breakfast, then headed to her area, undressed and slipped into bed.

Effie had to force herself to do her duties and then to remain in bed, because with every step, with every movement, with every thought, she was resisting the urge to go to him, to curl up like a kitten on the bed beside him, to offer him some warmth, to hear that deep liquid voice pour into her ears.

To share this night, not with a king, but with the man Zakari.

Concentrate!

Zakari was having trouble doing just that! The sun was high in the clear blue sky, his shadow invisible at his feet—feet that, even though it was only midday, kept willing him to return to her.

At first her chatter had irritated him. Her anxious face peering around the tent each evening as she awaited his return had gnawed at him. Her clumsy ways as she prepared his bath, her tall tales of her mother's time in the Aristo palace had, at first, irritated him. The way Effie described her mother, she sounded more like a princess than a mere maid.

Yes, at first it had irked him.

And yet, now…

He had come to look forward to it.

The day dragged on endlessly. It was still hours from sunset, and, though he tried to focus on the problems of the islands, his mind wandered. No matter how much he tried to clear his thoughts it was either his brother's image that danced before his eyes, or it was her face that drifted into focus… Her scent that seemed to lead him back long before sunset.

'You're early!'

Christobel would have been lying on a low sofa, reading trashy magazines, drinking wine, Zakari thought…yet here was Effie, rehanging the coloured drapes around the low cushions on the floor.

'I'm sorry you had to see the place like this, Your Highness.'

'Carry on.'

'I just took them outside to freshen them up,' Effie explained.

'It is no problem.' He was frowning slightly, but not because she was working. There was something different about her, something he couldn't quite place. She was on a small ladder and Zakari watched with more than idle interest as she stretched, her dress lifting, showing creamy, smooth white thighs, and Zakari felt his throat tighten a touch, could see the strain of the fabric over her large breasts, the curve of her round bottom as he stretched out on the cushions.

'So, how was your day?' She gave a little laugh as she hung the final drape. 'Not that it's any of my business.'

'It was…' Zakari pondered for a moment '…less than productive.'

'Oh!'

Her cheeks were pink from exertion, those blue eyes bluer somehow, like two glittering jewels, and her mouth soft and pretty.

How, Zakari thought to himself, could he not have seen her beauty?

And then Zakari felt his heart still for a fraction. As she stretched to arrange the drape Christobel's ill-fitting dress allowed a revealing glimpse of Effie's smooth underarms. His eyes once again ran down her legs seeing again the smooth skin there, the sheen of moisturiser now clearly evident. Only now he realised she had been playing with Christobel's things.

'Can I ask why?' Her question confused him; he was completely unable to recall what they had been discussing. 'You said your day had been less than productive.'

'Oh, that!' Zakari gave a quick nod, relieved she had not sensed his distraction, embarrassed, had he but known it, at almost being caught staring. 'I seem to be spending a lot of time thinking about my brother.' He watched her pause, her kind, worried face turning around. Her hair was tumbling out of its tie and long snaky curls danced around her slender neck. 'Thinking of the man he would be, had he lived.'

'That's because you spoke of him.'

'It is nice to remember.' Zakari gave a pale smile. 'It hurts, but it is good.'

'I'm so sorry for your pain,' Effie said, and Zakari knew that she meant it, knew that she offered so much more than a platitude. 'Does it ever lessen?'

He knew then she was asking for herself, about her own private pain, that she was so much newer on the path of grief than him.

'You learn to live with it. It does not diminish, but you learn to carry the load. And you will too,' he added.

'Thank you.' The small grateful smile she gave at his insight warmed him somewhere deep inside. Only Zakari didn't smile back, just held her gaze for a moment, waiting for her blush to deepen, for her to lower her eyes, for that moment of connection that always came so easily with women—that awareness that told him he was wanted.

Except it didn't happen. Instead she gave a wider smile and changed the subject. 'I will just finish off these, then I'll draw you a bath, but first I will get some refreshments…'

He gave a brief nod.

Lying back on the cushions, his tongue on the roof of his mouth as she worked just inches away from him, for the first time Zakari wondered about a woman.

Because till now he had always known the answer.

Always.

Always a woman wanted him, always there were signs; signs Zakari easily followed. He read women well—calm, neurotic, needy, wanton, he took pleasure in taming them all, interpreting involuntary signals, then homing in and claiming his triumphant prize. Rare was the woman who would refuse a king, yet they were the challenge Zakari relished the most. He loved the dance between a man and a woman, especially if she was unattainable, when he could use his sensuality, his prowess to reduce the most difficult woman to quivering jelly.

Only Effie was unreadable.

Was it curiosity that had had her toying with Christobel's things, or had it been for him?

'Done!'

As she came down the ladder for a second she was unsteady—well, not really, but it was excuse enough for Zakari to reach out his hand and steady her, to hold her as she took the last two steps.

'Thank you.'

His hand was on her wrist, her skin soft beneath his fingers, this smell catching him—not a hint of fragrance, just the scent of her alone, combined with the feel of her skin beneath his fingers, and there was his answer.

Though she seemed outwardly unperturbed he could feel her pulse flickering rapidly beneath his fingers, knew the contact had unsettled her, troubled her, but in the most primal of ways.

A bird had flown into the palace.

An ugly, small grey bird that caused momentary chaos.

Little Zafir was whooping with delight as he chased it, the maids running with brooms as the tiny bird fluttered and panicked, its terrified flapping leading it to the study, where it banged hopelessly against the glass doors.

Anya shooed the staff away, and told Zafir to quietly sit and observe while she addressed her eldest son.

'When trouble flies in, when people are running and shouting, you, Zakari, must stop the chaos with calm. Do not give in to the first response that comes to mind— do not run and chase along with the crowd. As a king, you must sit a while and observe. See how the palace that is so big to us is tiny and confining to him—see how he struggles to be free, but soon he will give in.' So they sat and waited till the tiny bird had found its resting place behind some books and slowly Anya parted them.

'He is there, Zakari. He is scared and petrified of you, yet he is still, so now you can help him.'

The bird was weightless in his thirteen-year-old palm. The ugly grey bird, when he looked closer, was actually many shades of silver, and as he held its terri-

fied body he could feel its helpless fear, the flutter of its tiny heart in his hand.

He took it to the garden, placed it beneath a tree and watched for twenty minutes as it sat stunned, and then it flew.

Zakari could feel her pulse beneath his fingers, fluttering just as the bird had, and though she was still, though Effie was outwardly unruffled, he knew she was terrified, could feel now the beats of her excitement—and suddenly Zakari wanted her to soar.

He felt the cool space as she reclaimed her hand and turned and smiled, her voice friendly and even, as with calm demeanour she denied what they both knew.

'I will prepare some refreshments.'

Her face was on fire as she fled into the kitchen area. Her wrist felt as if it had been scalded where Zakari had touched her and she was tempted to run it under cool water, only that wouldn't soothe the dangerous heat elsewhere…

The vast tent seemed tiny now, as if it were under a magnifying glass, as if the heat of the sun were concentrated on this one minute scrap of the desert.

Effie wanted her old job back. Wanted the familiar palace walls, her usual routines and the anonymity they brought. Wanted to be back where a maid wouldn't hold the spotlight of the king's gaze.

The desert played tricks on one's mind, Effie told herself, loading the tray as she willed herself calm—made you see things that weren't there…caused mirages to appear. That was what had just occurred, she insisted to herself as she carried the heavy tray through. Zakari hadn't been looking at her in *that* way.

Sheikh King Zakari Al'Farisi would never look at her with want in his eyes.

It was entirely irrelevant that she wanted him.

Kneeling down, she poured iced mint tea. Christobel's uniform on her was clearly way too small, the fabric straining over her curves, the top button impossible to do up, and as she bent forward she gave him a brief glimpse of her cleavage. Zakari's jaw tightened as he saw a flash of a chain around her neck, the weight of its pendant dragging it down, clasping it between her creamy breasts, and he wished his finger were that lucky stone, nestled in that sweet warmth, or his tongue, Zakari thought, flaring with lust. He was tempted to put his hand out, to stroke the back of her neck, to capture her cheek in his palm, only he knew then what her reaction would be…

It would terrify her.

'Join me,' Zakari instructed, despite the fact it was the afternoon and she would still have many duties to perform. 'Have some tea.'

She was trembling with nerves this time when she sat beside him, those blue eyes struggling to meet his as he attempted to put her at ease.

'Would it be decadent to build a pool in the middle of the desert?'

'Sinfully!' Effie smiled, as Zakari did the same.

'Shame!' Zakari shrugged. 'It is the only thing I sometimes miss when I am out here.'

As both their eyes simultaneously flicked away both knew he'd lied by omission.

'I love pools too!' Effie spoke too quickly, trying to fill in the suddenly awkward gap. 'Well, I love looking at them—the Calistan palace pool is just stunning, I remember my mother telling me about the pool at the Aristan royal lodge at Kionia.'

'I thought your mother worked at the palace?'

'She did.' Effie shrugged. 'Maybe she was sent there to clean one day. There is an infinity pool that looks out to the rough sea. My mother said it was the most amazing sight…'

Zakari just smiled at yet another extravagant tale. He knew she was talking rubbish—the pool had been commissioned by Queen Tia, when Princess Elissa, their youngest child, had been born and that would have been long after her mother had stopped working at the palace. It was just Effie's glorious imagination at work again. She must have heard about the pool and weaved it into her fanciful stories about her mother, and Zakari didn't mind a bit—still she made him smile and he liked hearing her talk.

At first it had annoyed him, now it soothed him and now he wanted to know *everything* about her.

'You are betrothed?'

'No…' She let out a shy giggle.

'You are twenty-five, though.' He watched her cheeks flush at his comment. Most poor women of Effie's age were already married and had children.

'I do not have family to arrange such things,' Effie answered, more than a touch embarrassed. 'I've been busy looking after my mother over the years, and, anyway, I don't have time for such things. It's hard enough working at the palace all day without having to come home and start over again.'

'That to you is marriage—being a servant?'

'I haven't much else to offer…' Effie shrugged.

'I disagree.' It angered him to hear her talk this way,

this low rumble of anger that slowly built inside him. Angry with himself too for the first impression he had had—she wasn't the dumpy, plain woman he had thought he had seen—with confidence, with guidance, she really could be very beautiful.

He saw again the curve of her breast straining in Christobel's tight clothes, her downcast eyes when she spoke to him, and there was a flash of something else when their eyes occasionally met that had Zakari pondering.

Lucky the man whom she gave her heart to, Zakari thought to himself.

'One day I might meet someone.' Effie shrugged. 'Some of the servants at the palace show some interest, but that is only because I have my own home… I know they are not really interested in me.'

'You should not talk about yourself like that.'

'How should I, then?'

'You should expect to be treated well.' It annoyed him that she shrugged. 'If your boyfriends have treated you poorly in the past, it is because you have allowed them to.'

Still she shrugged; still it irritated.

'Perhaps.'

'When a king offers advice, most people take it,' Zakari said tartly.

'Of course, Your Majesty!' Chastised, instantly Effie apologised. 'It is not that I disagree, it is more…' she shrugged *again*, only this time it didn't irritate '…there have been no boyfriends. If that day comes, I will take your advice—I am truly grateful for it. It is just, at the moment, marriage isn't something I dream of.'

'So what do you dream of?'

'I don't know…' Effie frowned in confusion.

'If not marriage…'

'To be happy, I suppose.'

'You are not happy.'

'I am…' She was really confused now, because she actually was happy—here, now, talking to him, being with him, for the first time since her mother's death, Effie was actually happy. Her eyes lifted to his, blinking as she admitted the truth she had just learnt herself. 'Right now I am happy.'

'Yet you don't have dreams?'

'Of course I do…' Effie blushed darker. 'But dreams are private, dreams are just that, dreams aren't real.'

'What do you dream of?' His eyes held hers. 'Tell me.'

'Tell you?'

'Tell me,' he said again as she hovered on the edge of indecision, unsure, so, so unsure whether to reveal her thoughts, ashamed that she was even considering it, yet Zakari took care of it for her. As if he could read her mind, he revealed it, or some of it. 'Do you dream of princes who will take you away from your job?'

'Don't be silly.' A soft smile played on her full lips, but her heart was hammering…

'Of what, then?' Zakari demanded, and there was no hope of even pretending this was idle conversation. His black eyes were boring into her, the air so thick with tension she was having trouble dragging it into her lungs. The flirting, the little teases she had ignored these past couple of days, had convinced herself were borne from her imagination, were all concentrated now into this one heady moment.

'I dream of kings…' Effie swallowed, biting down on her lip, having voiced her most private truth.

'Kings?' Zakari checked, a soft smile playing on his full mouth.

'One king,' Effie whispered as her eyes locked with his.

'And in your dream—does this king dress you in finery, does he lavish you with jewels?'

'No…' Her cheeks burnt under his scrutiny. 'That would be an impossible dream for a woman in my position.' However unwritten, there were the first etchings of a contract being drawn up and Effie knew that.

'What would you want from this king?' He saw a flash of tears in her eyes, saw the confusion buzzing in them, then she shook her head, breaking the spell and dispersing the thick hum of desire that hung in the air between them, but as she stood he knew she was dizzy.

'I must get on.'

How she longed for the palace, longed for walls to separate them, for people, for routine, but there was no escape here in the desert. Even though he ignored her at dinner, even though, this night, he didn't ask her to join him on the cushions, still there was no escape from the genie she had let out of the bottle, the knowledge that she had flirted, had let him glimpse her inner desires.

The night stretched endlessly. Sitting in the staff quarters, she read a book as she waited for Zakari to retire, then tidied up the living area before heading to bed herself, but sleep evaded her.

The night was sultry, and Effie lay awake in the oppressive heat with no escape from her thoughts.

Sex had never been at the top of her agenda—had never really been on her agenda at all. Her virginity hadn't been kept as some prize to give when the love of her life appeared, it was just something she had kept.

Aware she wasn't a classic beauty, she had assumed that was the reason that no man had ever made advances, but what was it that Zakari had said—that she should expect to be treated well? Maybe she could, if she just had a tenth of Christobel's confidence…or even an ounce of her experience!

Effie blushed in the dark at her own dangerous thoughts. Sex and romance had been but a distant dream, just a tiny occasional dance on the periphery of her existence. But since she'd been here, since she'd seen him so beautiful and naked, it had startled her into awakening. His image was one she couldn't banish from her mind.

Maybe she could have, had he not spoken to her.

Had he treated her as nothing more than a lowly maid, she could maybe have moved on, but lying in bed at night, each night, it was his face that drifted before her tightly closed eyes.

Lying there now, she thought of him and that intimate moment she had witnessed, those beautiful black eyes closed in bliss. As she saw again his fingers wrapped around his length her own thighs were heavy, and low, low in her stomach this dull ache throbbed. Dragging in a breath, she almost felt his hands on her waist, her hips. She had felt his eyes on her breasts that evening and as if in reflex her nipples stiffened at the memory as she guiltily explored her body, only through Zakari's eyes.

And then she stopped, a sob of frustration on her lips as she rolled over and willed sleep to come, scolding herself for even daring to imagine that a king could grace her dreams.

She willed it to be morning, when he would head out to the desert and she could breathe freely again.

CHAPTER THREE

EXCEPT the desert had other ideas.

Effie woke from a restless, thwarted sleep, to the screams and cries of desert winds.

Oh, she'd witnessed sandstorms from the safe confines of the palace, had gazed out of the windows in awe as the winds picked up the landscape and shifted it, and she had heard the tales and fables too.

That the screams of the wind were actually lost souls calling for company. Screams that sounded so real they would lure sane, rational people out from the safety of shelter to explore.

That the banshees would lure them to their death.

She hadn't believed the tales, but as the wind battered the tent, as it screamed its wild lament around them, Effie believed them now. Washing quickly, she tried to ignore them but every now and then she could have sworn she could hear a woman crying, screaming, calling and begging her for help.

'Damn!' Effie cursed as she saw her bra and knickers still soaking. In her frantic quandary last night, she'd forgotten to hang them up, and, given she hadn't packed for her time in the desert, there were only Cristobel's things to choose from.

New things, Effie realised as her shaking hands opened tissue paper. The King must give her an allowance, because no maid could afford silk and satin and velvet.

Slut's things, Effie thought, dropping them like hot coals on her bed when she saw the tiny knickers and decadent, lacy bras. Only her curiosity was again piqued, and, of course she couldn't serve the King breakfast without underwear, Effie told herself, gingerly picking up what appeared the safest option.

A white bra and knickers—only there was nothing virginal about them.

The tiny ribbons on the panties cut into her flesh and she could see the tiny remains she had left of her intimate curls through the flimsy fabric. And as for the bra...

The only thing she had in common with Christobel was a generous bust, but when she put it on the straps cut into her back and shoulders. Yet, as uncomfortable as it felt, she shivered in curiosity as she gazed at herself in the mirror. Her breasts had always been shoved into a sensible bra that served only to cover her, and did nothing to support her, but now they stood uplifted, giving her endless cleavage, clamping her mother's necklace in their grasp. She could see the pink of her areolae through the shamelessly sheer lace, see her hard nipples staring at the fabric, and Effie blinked at the changes such a small garment made to her body—for the first time she actually had a waist. Brushing her teeth, she saw her flushed cheeks and wild hair in the tiny mirror, and she dragged it back into a low ponytail, splashed her face with cool water, but nothing helped— the genie really was out of the bottle now and nothing could tame her wantonness.

Even pulling on her frumpy maid's uniform did nothing to calm her.

She knew.

Heading out to prepare his breakfast—Effie knew what she wanted.

Thoroughly untogether and jangling with nerves, she brought jugs of coffee and fruit juices to the table, spilling one and having to hastily clear the mess and replace the cloth, before Zakari came to eat.

Was it any wonder she was jumpy and unsettled? Zakari wouldn't be going out in the winds today. She could hear him now. Normally he went outside at sunrise and returned for his fatir, but this morning he was silent and thoughtful and just dizzied her brain more.

'Good morning, Your Highness.' Effie lowered her head as he entered the dining area. 'Did you sleep well?'

'No.' Zakari's voice was surly. 'Did you?'

'No,' Effie admitted, then flushed, remembering the reason she hadn't been able to sleep. 'The winds kept me awake.'

'The winds only started half an hour before dawn…' His eyes never left her burning face as he outed her. 'Perhaps there were other reasons you could not sleep.'

A screech shot from the desert, so loud it made her jump.

'When the wind hurtles through the canyons it makes these noises,' Zakari explained. 'Forget the tales you have been told.'

'It sounds so real, like a woman screaming…'

'Some winds sound like children laughing,' Zakari said, 'some like cats fighting. Do not let it play tricks with your mind. Don't even think of going out to investigate. You are only safe here.'

Except she didn't feel safe, but it wasn't the wind or Zakari she feared.

It was herself.

'I will take my breakfast in bed this morning…' His eyes left her face, then flicked down, only low enough to register the nervous swallow in her throat, then back up again, a glint of triumph in his eyes. 'You will serve it to me there.'

As Effie walked in with the tray they both knew that the one time she'd seen him on this bed, he'd been naked. And, even though he was covered to the waist now, Effie knew what lay under his silk sheets.

The tiny jewelled cup was rattling loudly on the tray as she lowered it, sick almost with terrified arousal as she placed the tray in his lap.

He could smell her want as she walked towards him, could taste it in the air he breathed. Zakari rarely bothered with kissing. It was boring and pointless and served no real purpose. Women wanted kisses, kings wanted sex…

Yet as she leant over to remove the coffee from the tray to place it at the bedside she was so jittery, if he told her to take off her dress, to join him, Zakari knew she would turn and run.

So, Zakari mused, he would deign to kiss her.

The bliss of his beard on her face was unsurpassed. It was just bliss, bliss, bliss. The soft weight of his mouth on hers didn't even make her jump, just this faint relief that caused tears to sting at her eyes as her mouth moved with his. She didn't know what to do with her breath, though, holding it in her mouth till she dared open it to let it out, her lips parting…and then she felt his tongue.

Cool and shocking in her mouth.

Deliciously shocking, though.

This wedge of muscle that stroked, that teased a little, then teased her some more. At first it was almost still, slipping slowly inside, and then it mingled, tasting her, stroking her, till finally she relaxed, till her mouth fully accepted him in a deep moist kiss that she never wanted to end.

And then he stopped.

Abruptly he stopped and looked at her. He had given her a taste; it was up to her to ask for more.

'Your dream is not so foolish.'

'No?' She shivered with indecision by his bed, part wanting to leap in, part wanting to run out.

'For one day at least we can make it real…'

'But, Your Highness…'

'You can call me Zakari if you return for my tray within five minutes…' His eyes glittered as they delivered his offer. 'If you do not return, Your Highness will leave the tray outside, and then I will remain here in bed, but then…' the image he conjured made her stomach tighten '…I am not to be disturbed.'

She fled to her bedroom and sat rocking with indecision on the bed. The banshees were screaming their warning outside, only she didn't want to listen, yet they wailed at her to be careful, not to be foolish, not to give herself to a man who could promise her nothing more than a few hours in his arms. Effie was suddenly acutely aware of her mother's jewel between her breasts, warning her, just as Zakari had, that this man would take her, then discard her.

But what a man!

Today, for one day, she could be a princess, could live the fairy tale.

With shaking hands she took off her necklace, like turning her mother's photo to the wall.

Zakari would never admit to sleeping with someone so lowly—and what future husband, if he did one day appear, would ever believe she had slept with a king?

He had given her five minutes to make up her mind. She was back within three.

'Take off your dress,' Zakari ordered as she entered.

Only that wasn't how she wanted it to be.

She wanted his kiss again, wanted him to undress her slowly beneath the safety of the sheets, but then, what did she know? Effie thought. What man would want her in her heavy white dress?

'Take off your dress!' Zakari said again, his impatience evident this time.

Each button she undid was humiliation itself, purgatory visited, but, dropping her dress to the floor, she was plunged straight into hell. Standing pale and big as his eyes roved her body, she was bitterly ashamed of her generous flesh, her arm moving to hide her flimsily covered breasts, her other hand trying to more suitably hide herself than did her panties.

But Zakari was entranced—she was more beautiful than he had ever imagined.

Magnificent actually.

Yet so painfully shy, so visibly, acutely awkward that something shifted inside him. The voice that had ordered her to undress delivered words more softly now.

'Effie, there is nothing more beautiful to a man than the flesh of an innocent woman...'

'Forgive me if I differ,' Effie responded in a shaking voice. 'Innocence is not always considered fetching these days.'

There was an element of truth to her words. She would be a clumsy, unskilled lover, not what he had considered he needed, his time too valuable, his needs too urgent, but, Zakari realised, today Effie and her precious innocence were exactly what he wanted.

'I will teach you.'

Sex had been his intention, but, seeing her so shy, Zakari was consumed almost by a sense of responsibility, the same sense of responsibility that greeted him each morning, that he lived with each waking moment. Only it was a responsibility he had never felt towards a woman, yet he felt it keenly now, wanting for Effie, this day, this time, this moment to be special. Deciding that for today at least her dreams would be made real.

He rose from his bed, and walked towards her.

Naked, erect and so potently beautiful, he stood in front of her as she wept in fear and lust and shame.

He took her by the hand and led her to his sleeping area—the bed was unmade, his bath not even run, the morning routine just gloriously abandoned. He could feel her shaking. Breathing in the intoxicating mixture of terror and want, he laid her down on the bed, then lifted the sheet over her, hoping it made her feel safer, watching her relax a touch as the silk fabric covered her, and he swore to himself that he would not be the one who removed it.

That it would be Effie herself.

This low thrill of excitement building as he made in that moment a decision that she, Effie, would be made love to as only a master in the subject could.

He gazed at her trembling mouth, could feel her clumsy, rigid in his arms, and instead of irritating him it excited him. There could be no gifts, no shows of affection after this day, but he would give her a greater gift instead—the thrills and secrets of her own body.

His finger traced her round cheeks, his thumb grazing her bottom lip, pulling down the plump flesh and releasing it. Then he lowered his noble head and his lips met hers, this mesh of flesh that for Effie was, at first, nothing but awkward.

His lips nuzzled hers, waiting for her to relax, waiting for the woman he had glimpsed a few moments ago to show herself again, impatient that she held back, then checking himself—this was Effie.

Zakari reminded himself.

His little silver bird.

His arms swept her right into him, wanting not just to arouse her, but to calm her.

He liked kissing her…as his mouth mingled with hers Zakari felt a surge of surprise.

All his life from childhood he had believed he hadn't liked apricots, and yet one day, inadvertently, he had taken one from a lavish fruited display as he worked, and he had found to his mild surprise as he bit into the velvet flesh and tasted the ripe fruit that he did like them after all. There was no mild surprise here though, just pleasure, *supreme* pleasure as on and on he kissed her, as he licked at her tongue, and as later he rained kisses on her face and felt her wriggle and curl in his arms.

Here in the magical desert, with no one but them, he initiated her to the secrets of her body and for Effie it was nothing short of wondrous.

Her hands at first had been clamped by her side, yet in moments they shot upwards, her fingers knotting into his silky hair as he kissed her. The scratch of his beard on her cheeks as his mouth pressed into hers hurt, yet it was a luscious hurt as his lips pressed harder.

Oh, and she learnt, *how* she learnt—that a kiss, that just a kiss could inflame her so, could inflame him too. That a kiss could have her wriggling out of the safe cocoon of the sheet because she wanted her skin next to him, that a kiss would have him pressing his heat into her stomach. That the thrill of a man's arousal just pressed against her could have her damp and have her pressing her own engorged flesh to his in a bid to calm him.

Shy at first, she had been stunned at his low, throaty moans as he ran his hands over her body, quivered in delight at his rampant approval.

And Zakari clearly approved.

Too often Zakari had found that a woman looked better dressed, whether it be in a designer gown, a well-fitted bra or a pretty flash of silk that covered her most secret place, or just heavy jewels around her throat carefully engineered to direct the eye.

Oh, women used them because they worked and gave teasing, revealing glimpses that let the imagination run riot.

And yet…

Too many times Zakari had felt hard borders of silicone on upright breasts, seen tiny creases of a cosmetic surgeon's scars and a manufactured belly button, or a crêpe neck beneath a choker, and these things did nothing to arouse him. Yet as Effie lay writhing in his arms, their absence aroused him now.

Here before him, Effie was what no woman before had managed. Better, far better naked, he realised as he took off her bra and slid her panties down over the generous curve of her hips.

Only now, under his sensual command, did her beauty truly reveal itself.

Against the dark silk sheets as he laid her onto the bed she was a delicious pillow of white skin, broken only by a delicate flush of pink on her cheeks that swept to her chest as his eyes bathed her with admiration. His mouth and tongue worked their languorous but definite way down her neck till they kissed her full breasts, flicking the nipples, then in turn taking them deep into his mouth and sucking slowly as Effie squirmed in pleasure. His fingers were pressing on her lips now and she sucked them into her mouth greedily, only stilling as his fingers left her mouth and his hand crept to her private place, moving again as tenderly he stroked her. She made a little gasp in her throat as his fingers worked their magic, and she wanted it to go on, didn't want him to stop, appalled when he knelt before her, when the rules of this very new game shifted, and he lowered his head between her legs.

Lowered his noble head and tasted her pretty pink flesh again.

Prepared her with his tongue.

And for Effie, as the first flash of embarrassment faded, as she closed her eyes and just lost herself to his silken touch, it was heaven.

His silky hair against her thigh, his beard teasing and scratching her swollen mound, the thick, wet, pressing weight of his tongue as he stroked her combined with his rhythmic massage of her breasts, was like being dragged down in a whirlpool of sensations. For a full moment she forgot to breathe as he took her ever deeper into this entrancing place.

And the noise.

How lacking her fantasies had been, how empty they were, without celebrating the pleasurable, sensual noise that a man and woman created when skin and membranes danced.

This delicious noise that only they two made—this lavish, greedy feast of indulgence and shameless want that could not be contained as he took her to new pleasures.

And, for Zakari, never had there been more pleasure in giving and in feeling her unfurl beneath him. The sweet taste of her, the breathless, throaty, lavish attention, for a moment threatened to overwhelm him, his erection so fierce, his climax so close, he wanted to take her right then. He closed his eyes, waiting for it to abate, but it was hopeless, her image branded on his mind as she moved beneath him and he knew he had to have her now.

Resting back on his heels, he stared down at her moist and so ready.

Always he sheathed himself—aware how women coveted his valuable seed. It was unthinkable to consider otherwise, but seeing her glistening and pink, her virgin flesh, moist and waiting, he was kneed in the groin with a want, a desire, to feel her precious untouched skin around his.

'When—' Zakari himself was having trouble speaking, his breath catching, making his voice low and harsh '—is your time?'

When she didn't immediately answer, he asked her

again. 'You cannot get pregnant! I need to know, when was your time?'

She never discussed such things with anyone, let alone a man, and Effie screwed her eyes closed as she answered such a personal question.

'It just finished.' The tip of his impressive erection hovered and teased the jewel of her clitoris.

'Just?' Zakari checked.

'Yesterday.'

The devil on his shoulder had never been louder or more willingly heeded. If she had just finished they surely had a few days, surely not…his mind told him, but surely yes, the devil argued. He was at her entrance now, he could feel her slippery and warm beneath him, wanted to feel her for just a little while longer, and he'd be careful, Zakari assured the fading sensible voice.

'Will it hurt?'

'No.' His voice was suddenly tender; he would not hurt her. His fierce erection was nudging her entrance, and yet he held back, just the tip of him entering her innocent resistance, moistening her barrier with a rush that was unexpected.

Steady—Zakari said it to himself as tenderly he probed, one step forward, then he took two back, till she begged that he deepened, his erection salivating at the feast ahead.

The path of resistance was made no easier by her throaty gasps, and then she let out just a tiny sob as he parted her innocence. He waited, waited for her to adjust to the sensation of him inside her, tender words spilling unchecked and unheeded from his mouth, till Effie relaxed again, till he was led in deeper by the delicious, spongy pull of her intimate vice…

Enough reward, Zakari told himself, yet it felt divine without the usual constraints, with her so oiled and willing; he wanted to remain, wanted to explore for just a moment longer this sweet uncharted territory. She was moving with him and he was so close to coming, he knew he must cease, yet he wanted to stay and play a little while more yet. Looking down, he could see his length moving in and out of her, could see her rising to meet each thrust, and it was so erotic, if he were to linger and gaze on for even a moment longer it would be over, so instead he lay over her, sliding deep inside her.

He could sustain, Zakari told himself. That when he was as close as this, dammit, he could hold back.

He really should sheath himself. As he moved deep within her, as he kissed her face, her neck and as her fingers dug into his buttocks, her legs locked over his, the soles of her feet digging into his calves, then up to his thighs, Zakari knew he should stop a moment and protect himself, yet he didn't want to. A million slivers of silver had surely already moistened his path, an unreasonable voice pointed out, surely it was already too late for concern, surely, just this once, he could allow himself the full extent of this rare pleasure.

This shy, sweet woman he had first led to his bed was unleashed beneath him now, sobbing out as she came, her fingers digging into him as he took her to that wondrous place. He could feel her body frantic now, the pulse of her orgasm everywhere around him, in her thighs that gripped him, in her arms that held him, and in the arched neck that he kissed. It was an orgasm so intense that it consumed him just as it consumed her. Zakari shuddered in blessed relief as he shot deep within her, and if it was forbidden, with every last pulse, it was utterly without regret, just the headiest of release, the bliss not just of his orgasm or hers, but *theirs*.

What *they* had somehow achieved.

He lay on top of her for the longest time afterward, still deep inside her. Zakari relished every fading flicker of her orgasm, feeling their cool sweat mingling, their hearts beating a frantic race then steadying, but he was dizzy.

Dizzy as still his head lay in her neck, her damp curls on his face, and he inhaled the intoxicating scent of lovers entwined, proud and safe in the knowledge that her first time had been wonderful. He felt this strange…peace, almost, descending as his mind wandered to the strangest of places—pausing for a curious moment—where it almost felt as if it had been his first time too.

He never talked after sex.

Just slept, or watched, usually bored, as his bed partner dressed and left.

Only today was different. The bed was warm, her body so soft, as the winds screamed their fury at what had just taken place.

'The banshees are cross!' Effie giggled. 'They warned me not to do it, you know?'

He laughed; for the first time in the longest time, he actually laughed.

'Are you glad that you did?' Zakari faced her and she turned side-on and they faced each other.

'Utterly!' Effie breathed, because she was. Without a trace of regret she smiled over to him. One perfect day was more than enough for Effie, and it had been perfect—her body felt different, warm and alive and, thanks to his lavish compliments during their lovemaking, for the first time in her life she felt beautiful. 'This has been the best day of my life. I'll never be scared of the wind again; for the rest of my life, every time I hear it I'll remember feeling like this.'

Her eyes dragged down his body, could see the scratches of her nails and the bruises her lips had left. She couldn't believe the passion he had evoked in her, the woman he had made her. And there, resting, sleeping on his thigh, was the most beautiful sight of all, and she wanted to disturb it, wanted to stroke it.

'It's so beautiful.' Effie sighed.

And he watched, willed her with his mind to be gentle with her fingers, his breath catching as she was. Her supremely tender fingers were soothing almost as they greeted his tumescent length, the tip of her finger slowly, deliciously, tracing a thick vein. 'You did all those glorious things for me, and yet I did nothing for you.'

'You did plenty…' Zakari smiled, growing in her gentle hand. 'But even so…' Effie stared, her heart stilling when Zakari continued as the terms of the contract suddenly shifted.

'We've still got tonight.'

Why not? Zakari said to himself as her eyes widened. Why should she not have one night of perfection?

She was kissing his nipple now.

This, the wanton, sensual woman he had created.

Snaky dark ringlets danced on his chest as her tongue searched and probed, and her mouth paid him minute attention.

His fingers entwined in her hair and he could feel himself grow so hard he almost begged her mouth to follow his mind, to move her lips from the pleasure she was bestowing and deal with the rather desperate arrival.

Only there would be more pleasure in waiting.

He lifted her chin up, stared into her blue eyes as he resisted the lure of her mouth.

'Dress for me…'

'Sorry?'

'Tonight—you will dress for me, like a princess.'

'I have nothing that fits,' Effie said, perplexed.

'You have your pick of fabrics.' He gestured to the organza, silk and velvet drapes. 'Christobel's make-up….'

Embarrassed, Effie turned on her side facing away from him. For a moment she had felt beautiful—oh, she had known it couldn't last, but had hoped for a few more moments before normality invaded.

'Tonight we will feast…'

His mouth was on her shoulder, kissing away the sudden knots of tension there. 'Go now, and prepare, and I will dress for you too…for tonight at least, you will be treated as royal.'

She had never dressed for any man—let alone a king…

But it felt wonderful.

A dark purple velvet drape, the depth of colour exquisite, was her choice of fabric for tonight, and every luxury was at her disposal to fashion the material into the gown of her dreams. Simple seams and a long split at the side left a teasing glimpse when she walked, the demure scoop she had attempted for the neckline had turned into a rather magnificent empress line, yet the effect was stunning as she slithered it over her head, watching, as if by magic, her figure transformed from nondescript to hourglass.

He had given her access to his mistress's area—and Effie had gasped as he'd let her in.

'All these things…' Antique, full-length mirrors glittered a welcome, along with tiny glass bottles that promised to transform.

'Use anything…' Zakari smiled, handing her an intricately carved silver box. 'There are jewels…'

'My mother has a jewellery box, just like this, at home…'

'This is eighteenth century…'

'Of course, it must be a replica,' Effie conceded, tracing the familiar pattern with her nails, sure it must be a sign that her mother would, if not approve, then understand, then opening the box and gazing at the jewels, too engrossed to notice Zakari's frown.

When he left her alone, Effie found, if she positioned them correctly, the mirrors did amazing things for her confidence. The dressing table was a delight in itself—awash with gleaming hair clasps, heavy silver combs and brushes, and velvet boxes that brimmed with make-up. It actually reminded her of her mother's dressing table—the pretty glass-stoppered bottles filled with scents, the array of boxes filled with jewels and make-up.

Sitting on a stool, Effie didn't know where to start. Holding the ivory make-up brushes and staring at the palette that would hopefully transform her, she truly didn't know where to start.

Less is more.

She could hear her mother's voice, remembered a time long ago when her mother had been ill, but had still insisted on going out, how she had instructed Effie to do her make-up.

Covering her dress, first Effie dusted her face with loose powder, then swirled a brush in a tiny silver box that held velvet brown eye shadow—her mother's favourite colour for accentuating her blue eyes...

And it worked.

As did the kohl and the mascara. Effie stared at two blue jewels that glimmered in the mirror before her, excitement mounting as she dusted her cheeks with pretty pink, then rouged her lips, then, deciding it was too much, rubbed it off.

She was feverish with excitement. Scooping up her heavy brown curls, she twirled them with inexperienced fingers, but the banshees must have forgiven her because with just one grip of a silver clasp they held in place, just a few stray ringlets trailing down her neck and falling over her left eye.

The least vain of people, she was shocked when she stared into the dusky mirror, shocked by the beautiful woman she saw—the sensual being he had made her. Pulling the stoppers out of bottle after bottle, she took for ever to make her choice, inhaling each fragrance deeply, each scent so potently divine. At the second-last bottle the choice was made, the heady notes of musk and amber the perfect match to her mood, and Effie rubbed the glass stopper on her pulse points, remembering every kiss he had placed there as she did so, and hoping for more of the same.

She felt no shame.

Not a single jot as she dressed for her man.

So much so that she retreated to the staff quarters and took her mother's necklace from the tissue she had wrapped it in and boldly clipped it on. The heavy pink jewel looked stunning settled in her cleavage and somehow, Effie knew, she now had her mother's blessing in this—her virginity gone to the very best of causes.

She would feast with Zakari and then they would make love.

Tonight was hers.

CHAPTER FOUR

SHE was different, so very different from the sleek,
groomed women Zakari was becoming too used to.
Effie expected nothing from him, which, he reflected,
made him want to do things for her.

Different things, like stand before a mirror and shave.

Normally he returned to the palace from the desert
unshaven, yet for the first time in days Zakari shaved—
for the first time in fact, Zakari shaved himself!

He applied cologne and chose his robe with more
care than usual—black, with gold braid—enjoying the
game for as long as it could last. These past few hours
had proven just the elixir he needed after the tumultu-
ous months and it never entered his noble head that he
might be dressing to impress!

But something irked.

She had opened that jewellery box with ease—with
practised ease, Zakari had noted. Which meant little
alone, except it was a difficult clasp; he knew that,
because many women had asked his assistance, and yet
Effie had popped it open with one practised turn.

A cheap replica didn't normally stretch to such
nuances.

And then there was her mother's recollection of the pool at Kionia. He had put it down to a flight of Effie's imagination at the time, but now?

In his search for the jewel, he had studied the rumours that Aegeus had taken a palace maid as a lover, yet despite following that lead his search had turned up nothing. Either the rumours were false or Aegeus had covered his tracks well.

But why would he? Zakari reasoned.

There was no real scandal attached to a prince or king accepting the warmth of a woman's body—Zakari was living proof of that. Scandal only abounded when emotions were involved…

When kings or princes looked after the women who kept them warm.

The edge of his mouth curved in an iniquitous smile—there would be no problem getting Effie to open up to him.

But there was no rush; he would take his time. Tonight, duty was also going to be a pleasure.

As Zakari headed out from his quarters he surveyed the table she had prepared. Effie had been busy! It was laden with delicacies, the crystal glasses gleaming along with the silverware in the candlelight, the air fragrant with incense. There was nothing for him really to do, yet he headed to the empty kitchen, adding his own finishing touch to the feast, then smiling as, shy, nervous yet incredibly, breathtakingly beautiful, Effie walked in.

How, Zakari begged to himself as she stood for a nervous moment, could he have not seen her beauty?

How, that first day she had arrived, could he have even entertained feeling disappointed?

Regal—it was the first word that came to his mind.

The purple velvet that sheathed her body showed off her stunning curves to perfection, her dark wavy hair was piled on top of her head, gleaming ringlets framing her pale face, and all Zakari could think was, as gorgeous as it looked, all he wanted to do was take it down, to unclip each curl and run it through his fingers one by one. Those stunning, piercing blue eyes were nervous as they sought his reaction, and he felt something else too—a stir of something unfamiliar inside him as he registered the approval in her eyes: she approved of him.

'You look beautiful.' It should have been his line, but that it was hers swelled that unfamiliar feeling in his chest. He didn't recognise it as pride, pride that his efforts had been noted, as confident now under his gaze she walked over to him. Her fingers traced his now smooth chin. 'And you smell divine!'

'You do too.' He took her cool cheeks in the palms of his hand and kissed her.

She was shaking with nerves, yet still she was bold for him, and that touched him. His hands held her shoulders, his eyes holding hers for the longest time—stunned at the magic they had created this day and looking forward to the magic they would create tonight.

And then his heart stopped.

Because there between her heavy white breasts, glittering and gleaming in the candlelight, was the answer he had been seeking for so long, the diamond he had prayed these last days for his land to return to him.

Never had the desert failed him.

And despite his doubts, it hadn't failed him now. His fingers slowly traced her neck, then picked up the heavy pink stone, his face expressionless as finally he held the jewel he had sought for so long. His mind was whirring. Here was the reason he had not been able to focus—the desert had sent the winds, the desert had continually sent him back to her, back to the stone, back to all he had been seeking.

'This necklace is beautiful…' He was having trouble keeping his voice even. Maybe she had found it when dressing, maybe one of his relatives had perhaps left it forgotten in a jewel box…

'Thank you.'

"Where…' he cleared his throat '…did you find it?'

'Find it?' His eyes jerked up at the question in her voice. 'I didn't find it. It's mine.'

'Yours?'

'It's my favourite thing…' Effie smiled, reclaiming the jewel from his grasp and, holding it between finger and thumb, she gazed at it fondly. 'It's probably just glass, not worth a bean, but it means the world to me.' She let the diamond drop, and it nestled in its resting place between her creamy bosoms. His eyes were drawn to its magnificence, the candlelight making it glimmer and shine as only a diamond could, and he felt awash with fear almost that she had this in her possession and was completely unaware of its importance… 'I wear it all the time.'

'You didn't earlier,' Zakari pointed out. 'I'm sure I would have noticed.'

He saw her cheeks pink, a tiny shy smile dancing on her full lips as she answered. 'It didn't seem right to, given what we were doing… It was my mother's, you see—she left it to me.'

There was a frantic conversation going on in his head, warning him, alerting him, to tread carefully, but not by a flicker did he betray his anxiety, his expression nothing more than mildly curious as he again picked up the jewel between his thumb and finger, then, holding it in the palm of his hand, he examined it closely and for Zakari there was absolutely no doubt—his search was finally over.

Again the desert had delivered, his distraction these past days *had* been merited—it hadn't been Effie clouding his mind, it had been the desert guiding him, leading him back to the Stefani diamond.

Now, all he had to do was claim it.

'Sit…' Dropping the stone, he watched as it fell back against her pale skin, his eyes dragging back to hers. They sat on low cushions, Effie moving to serve the food. 'Allow me…' He poured her the champagne.

'Aren't you having one?'

'I don't drink…' Zakari explained. 'It does not mean that you cannot.'

'I've never had champagne.'

'Enjoy, then!'

He watched her take a tentative sip.

Watched as a flood of pink soon warmed her cheeks.

'You said your mother left you the necklace.'

'She did.'

'And your father…'

The blush that spread across her face had nothing to do with the champagne… Her beautiful blue eyes suddenly downcast, the candlelight cast dark shadows on her cheeks, making her eyelashes impossibly long.

'I don't have a father.'

'They broke up?' he asked and she gave a small jerking nod.

'Do you ever see him?'

'No.' Effie didn't like where this conversation was leading. She wanted romance, she wanted what they had once had, yet Zakari was grilling her as if she were sitting some sort of test.

'Have you ever seen him?'

Effie shook her head. 'Can we talk about something else, please?'

'I want to get to know you…' Though Zakari flashed a smile it didn't quite meet his eyes and the tone of his voice reminded Effie unequivocally that she was being spoken to by the King. 'So you never saw him? But surely he supported your mother…'

'They broke up before I was born,' Effie gulped.

'Do you know his name?'

Her cheeks were on fire, tears flashing in her eyes as shame swept over her. 'No!' The word was a mixture of a sob and a shout, her frustration not just at Zakari's line of questioning, but at her mother's vagueness over the years. The one piece of information she had so desperately sought from her mother had constantly been denied her, and it hurt and shamed her even now. 'She said that she had fallen in love, but had known from the start that it could never last. I think he must have been married or something…' A solitary tear rolled down her plump cheek. 'So, no—I don't know who my father is.'

Zakari could see her discomfort and distress and chose not to pursue it.

For now.

Aegeus… He topped up her champagne, then took a long drink of iced water. His dark eyes were black with hatred as he thought of the man who had treated his stepmother so cruelly—a hatred that, for now, Effie must not see.

How had he not worked it out before?

There had been more than just forbidden emotions involved—here in front of him was the result of that forbidden union.

She was Aegeus's spawn!

'Is everything okay, Zakari?' Effie checked, wiping her tear away with the back of her hand. She'd been longing for this night, but since they'd sat down all it had been was question after question. The tenderness of before was markedly absent and Zakari seemed different somehow; though he was talking to her, she could sense his distraction.

'Of course…' He forced a smile, saw the tension in her features and quickly moved to right it. 'How could it not be?'

Regal. When he had seen her dressed, her hair glossy, her face made up, it had been the first word that had come to mind—and with good reason.

Royal blood flowed through her veins.

No wonder the old bastard had died of a heart attack, Zakari thought darkly. No doubt Aegeus had realised that his putrid secrets were about to come spewing out.

Revenge. Zakari's smile was genuine now as again he topped up her glass. He had known it was close, but finally it was actually here.

With the jewel now his, he could rule both Calista and Aristo.

Once the jewel *was* his, Zakari reminded himself, his tongue on the roof of his mouth as he pondered his next move. The answer came to him in a trice.

'Marry me.' It was not a question—kings did not have to ask twice, so why was she smiling and shaking her head?

'Don't be ridiculous!'

'I have never been more serious.'

'Of course you're not—' Effie smiled '—but it *has* been nice to pretend for a while.'

'Effie, I do not joke about such things—I am serious.' He watched her eyes dart, saw her face pale as she realised that he was. 'That is the reason for all the questions tonight—you will understand I need to know your history if I am to take you as my bride.'

'We can't…' She gave a nervous laugh. 'I am a palace maid—the people would never accept me…' Flustered now, she stood up, the game over, the fantasy ruined, now that he'd taken it too far.

'I am King of Calista,' Zakari warned. 'I get what I want.'

Yet still she shook her head, half walking, half running from his table, and had there been a flicker of doubt as to her status, for Zakari it was extinguished then.

Royal blood *did* flow through her veins—there was an innate strength about her—and Zakari faced a fresh challenge now to convince her to be his wife.

And if there was one thing Zakari relished, it was a challenge.

'These days with you…' he caught her shoulder as she made to leave '…have been the happiest I have known. Our lovemaking, you cannot deny it was special—you bring me peace…'

'Special!' Effie gaped at him. Today she had come alive, her whole body, her life, her soul even, felt different. As wondrous as it had been, though, as much as she might think she loved him, she had never expected that love to be reciprocated. It had never once entered her head that their time together had been as magical for

Zakari as it had been for her, that he might feel the same. 'It was more than special. It was everything! More than anything I had dreamed possible...'

'Tell me...' Zakari implored. 'Tell me how I made you feel.'

'Beautiful,' Effie breathed, lost in his gaze, dizzy with the turn of events.

'Loved perhaps?' he said softly.

He saw her blink rapidly, saw her throat tighten as she took in his words, saw the beautiful jewel between her breasts—and knew it was now his.

'You love me?' Effie frowned.

'And you love Calista,' Zakari continued softly, silkily evading answering. 'You love the people of Calista. Effie, with you beside me, with you as my wife, I *know* I will be a better king.' He wasn't lying—though Zakari's version of honest differed from most! 'With you as my wife I will be a better ruler for the people—for *all* of the people.'

'Me?'

'You.'

'But, do you love me?'

Why should it matter? Bemused, Zakari stared down at her. He was offering marriage, for this palace maid to be the King's wife—every want, every need would be catered for. What was this love she demanded? This love that his brothers spoke of, the same love that saw Prince Sebastian renounce his right to the throne.

'Do you love me, Zakari?' she said again, and Zakari knew what his answer must be, knew for the sake of his people *this* lie was merited.

'I love you.' His voice was hoarse, the words unfamiliar. It was such a strange, strange thing to utter, but feeling her soften beneath his fingers, witnessing the magical effect of his words fade the trouble in her eyes, Zakari wielded his new power—an abracadabra that had opened her heart. When next he spoke his words were softer, pulling her towards him, and this time there was no resistance.

'I love you, Effie.'

He kissed her trembling mouth, his hand snaking around the back of her head, and then blazing a trail with his fingers, stroking her throat as skilfully he kissed her.

And Effie could barely breathe. The magnitude of what he was offering, that she would be the King's bride, didn't spin her world, but that he felt it too, that the love she felt for Zakari was being returned tenfold.

'Marry me.'

That Zakari loved her made the impossible easy. Effie gasped her acceptance as, dinner forgotten, he slipped her out of her dress, out of her shoes, out of her underwear, till she stood before him naked, wearing just her mother's necklace, giving him a stunning view of what he treasured the most... The Stefani diamond.

She saw the flash of approval in his eyes as they roved her breasts, and mistook it as lust for her.

'Soon...' His mouth worked her throat, her neck, her breasts, his fingers holding a different prize now and how right it felt to possess it. 'We will marry soon, before you have time to change your mind.'

'Why would I change my mind?' Effie gasped. His mouth was sucking her nipple now; her fingers were in his hair as he adored her all over again.

Sheikh King Zakari Al'Farisi loved her. It was more than she'd ever dared to dream.

'Why would I change my mind, when we love each other?'

CHAPTER FIVE

'You do not have to marry her, Your Highness.' Hassan, his chief advisor, delivered the news with a smile. Since the helicopter had landed at the palace Effie, under Zakari's brisk instruction, had been swept away to the royal quarters by bewildered staff. His aides and legal team had been huddled for hours in urgent talks as Aarif held the same urgent talk with his eldest brother, Zakari.

Aarif and his wife, Kalila, divided their time between Hadiya and Calista and were here now to prepare for a charity polo match that would be held in three weeks. A wedding, the King's wedding, no less, had not been on their agenda.

'Do not rush into this, Zakari,' Aarif pleaded. 'I understand about the jewel, about your desire to rule both Calista and Aristo, but to marry her...' Aarif shook his head. 'A few months ago, I would not even question your decision; marriage to me was about union, about duty, about a fitting bride—'

'She will be fitting,' Zakari interrupted, 'once she has been suitably taught and groomed.'

'You do not understand the point I am making,' Aarif refuted. 'You see how much happier I am?' He only continued when Zakari, after a brief hesitation, gave a terse nod. 'It was all about duty for me too—no pleasure. Now, with Kalila I am happy, I am playing my first polo match in a few weeks, I am doing things, for me…'

'I am the King,' Zakari retorted because, as close as Aarif could come to understanding, as a prince, he never fully could. 'My first duty is to my people.'

Aarif screwed his eyes closed and rested his head in his hands for a moment. Zakari could see the savage scar on his face, the remnants of the rope burns on his wrists, and understood Aarif's point; to see his brother, who had been so miserable, so riddled with guilt, finally at peace brought immense joy to Zakari—except the same rules didn't apply to him. His first duty wasn't to himself, it was to his people. 'You have a right to be happy, Zakari,' Aarif insisted.

'I will be,' Zakari said, 'when the jewel is safely returned, when I rule the Kingdom of Adamas—then, I will be happy.'

'I'm not talking about duty…' Aarif argued, and though he knew it was hopeless to try and persuade his brother when his mind was made up, still he tried. 'Kalila and I wanted you to be the first to know—she is expecting a baby…'

A smile broke on Zakari's face. 'You are going to be a father?' Seeing Aarif, who had struggled so much, so alive and happy, Zakari embraced him. 'This is wonderful news.'

'I want this for you too!' Aarif pleaded. 'I don't want you to live in a marriage of convenience or duty, Zakari. I want you to feel the happiness love brings. Life is too short for it all to be about duty and power. Listen to what the advisors say—there are surely other options.'

There were.

'The jewel belongs to the palace. Aegeus, technically, had no right to give it to her,' Hassan explained as Aarif and the aides smiled at the good news. 'We will, of course, offer a generous payment for her distress at losing what she thought was her mother's necklace. However, as we will clearly explain, it never actually belonged to her mother—which means in turn it does not belong to Effie Nicolaides.'

It was the first time he had heard her surname. The palace maid they were discussing was becoming more and more of a person as with every passing word Hassan dismissed her as less.

'If she argues, or protests too loudly, we can demand the sale of her home to go some way to covering the cost of the jewels her mother has sold over the years.'

'It might not be so straightforward…' Zakari responded calmly, though his stomach was churning, imagining Effie's reaction to the news, imagining these suits that sat before him intimidating her into submission.

'Then it is our job to make it straightforward.' Hassan smiled. 'You do not have to concern yourself again with her, Your Highness.'

'I slept with her.'

'No problem…' Hassan didn't flinch at the news—half his job seemed to involve sending flowers and trinkets to the King's ex-lovers. Occasionally he had to handle a threat to sue when a particularly bitter ex went to the newspapers in Aristo with her story—the Calistan journalists wouldn't dare print it. Not that the scandalous gossip that sometimes flared dinted Zakari's popularity; if anything it inflamed it. 'I will talk with her myself,' Hassan crooned. 'Perhaps we could arrange a nice necklace as a suitable replacement. A personal gift from you would, I'm sure, help soothe raw wounds! And naturally we will have her moved from the palace. You will not have to face her again.'

They had it all worked out, Zakari realised, except for one small detail!

'I slept with her without protection.' Zakari remained supremely calm as the meteorite hit the room. Hassan's eyes practically bulged as he digested the news—it was unheard of, just unheard of for a man of Zakari's status to even think of sleeping with a woman without taking the necessary precautions! The legal advisors whispered furiously amongst themselves, and Aarif closed his eyes and ran a worried hand over his forehead as Zakari spoke assuredly on. 'It would complicate matters enormously if we were to find out in a few weeks' time that she was pregnant.' Zakari's haughty voice broke the frantic chatter. 'Arrange the papers immediately. We will be married before sunset.'

Staff abruptly dismissed, Zakari sat with his brother.

'What were you thinking?' Aarif's voice was hoarse with shock. He, as much as Zakari, knew that sex without protection, for a man of their ilk, was just unthinkable.

'Clearly, I wasn't thinking at the time.' Zakari gave a dry smile as he stood up. 'I have made my bed, now I have to lie in it with her…'

The only thing was as Zakari stalked out to the sound of his brother offering his sympathy, as he swept past his worried staff now huddled in the corridor, as the palace shot into frenzied action to prepare for the ceremony, the only person who wasn't fazed, the only person who wasn't daunted by the prospect, was Zakari himself.

Lying in bed with Effie would, he knew, be a pleasure.

* * *

Instead of entering the staff quarters, Effie had been whisked away to a private suite where she had sat nervously for a couple of hours, until Zakari had swept into the room and told her the plans.

They were to be married that day.

There would be a private ceremony at the palace, Zakari had rapidly explained, followed by a formal ceremony in thirty days' time, where the people would officially welcome her.

For now it was about making things legal, he had added, before abruptly removing himself from her quarters, leaving Effie mouthing like a goldfish. Endless questions swirling in Effie's mind were all put on hold as staff suddenly appeared, bathing her, arriving with robes and dresses, fiddling with her hair and applying her make-up, all the while talking in hushed tones.

There was no sense of comradeship—no smiles or congratulations that one of *them* was about to break ranks and marry the King, because Effie wasn't even one *of* them.

The royal dressers and handmaidens reigned supreme over a mere palace maid and Effie could see doubt in their eyes, the incredulity breaking into their voices at times—two of the younger maids even hastily smothered a giggle when they dressed her.

Staring at her reflection in the mirror, once they had finished, all Effie wanted to do was weep—it all looked wrong.

They had straightened her hair, her make-up was too severe and the white candlewick robe, though beautiful, was too jewelled and too fussy for her heavy figure.

She was a blushing bride, for all the wrong reasons. She was led through the palace and into Zakari's vast study; dark rugs scattered the floor and an imposing desk was the centrepiece where several men sat, staring solemnly as she entered. The French windows were open, and the heady scent of the ornate gardens filling the room added the only soothing touch to her pounding senses, especially when her gaze fell on her groom.

He looked stunning.

Sheikh King Zakari Al'Farisi took her breath away as she shyly walked over to him. Dressed in the olive military uniform, medals from his exemplary service gleaming, his legs encased in long boots, a silver sword at his side, his head covered in the traditional black and white keffiyeh, he was as imposing as he was beautiful.

And he loved her, Effie reminded herself, clutching her mother's jewel and wishing she could be here to offer support now, because she was truly terrified. How she longed for him to take her in his arms, to whisper words of reassurance, but all he did was nod a brief greeting as she stood humbly by his side.

'There are some formalities we have to take care of…' Zakari gestured that she sit, then did the same, followed by the many men in the room. An array of documents were spread on the heavy table in front of them. 'As King, you will understand that even a whirlwind marriage like ours comes with an inevitable amount of paperwork that must first be taken care of?'

'Of course.'

He hadn't commented on her looks, had barely given her a glance as she had entered and his austere, formal voice was doing nothing to quell her nerves.

'Normally talks would have been conducted with your father,' Zakari explained. 'Obviously that is not possible, so I have done my best on his behalf to see that you will always be well looked after. We have to sign these papers before a judge.'

'Looked after?' Effie frowned. She would be his wife—what more could she want?

'There is the question of *mahr*…' Effie's frown melted away. She knew a little about *mahr*—a dowry that was paid to the wife. Zakari really was looking after her; she wouldn't have even thought to ask… 'This is your personal allowance and this will be your wardrobe allowance. Of course if you need more that will not be a problem, these are just details that must be addressed…' Zakari showed her the figures that made her eyes water. 'Then there is *muta'akhir*…' He saw her frown reappear. 'If we were to divorce—this is the post-divorce dowry, what you would receive from me…'

'Can I read it?' She heard a small cough from one of his aides, saw his eyes flash, and she understood it was no doubt irregular. They probably thought she couldn't read, but her mother had taught her well and she wanted to read the document before she signed anything. It was only Zakari who didn't seem fazed by her request.

'Of course.' He flashed a thin smile. 'Take your time.'

There were reams of papers—her title, her status, all outlined in minute details, yet that was a mere fraction of it. Her rights, their children's rights, were all outlined and Effie felt her throat tighten, the magnitude of what was taking place just starting to dawn.

'Sheikha Stefania of Calista….' Effie gulped as she read on… Yes, he had looked after her, because even if they were to divorce, which was unheard of, and for Effie, unthinkable, still she would have a luxury home near the palace, still she would be paid an exceedingly generous allowance, and she would have full access to the royal princes and princesses they might one day bear, though they would be raised in the palace...

'You will own my necklace?' Effie did a double take as she read through the carefully worded jargon. 'Why would you want my mother's necklace?'

'I had to let them know your assets.' Zakari flicked his hand dismissively. 'There had to be some division of assets to show your commitment to the marriage...'

'But even so...' Effie protested, clutching the pendant in her hand and shaking her head. 'It was my mother's gift to me when she died!'

'You have a property also,' Zakari explained rationally, 'and all the furnishings in it. I did not want to put that, I know it means a lot to you... You said the necklace was worthless—it is merely a technicality...'

'Of course...' He *was* looking after her, Effie reasoned. The King would never need her home, yet Zakari had understood how precious it was to her... Her fingers held the stone in her hand, and Effie realised how silly she was being, wavering over a stupid piece of glass. As if Zakari would ever want it...as if there would even be a divorce...

He loved her, Effie assured herself, reliving the words he had uttered over and over again, and like a balm they soothed her as she picked up the pen.

It was, as he said, a mere technicality.

'Where do I sign?'

'Not yet...' The door opened and Aarif and Kalila entered. Aarif was dressed in the same military uniform as his brother and was holding his wife Kalila's hand and Effie wished that Zakari would hold hers. Kalila was dressed in a pale lilac chiffon dress, her hair swept back from her face, and she looked pale and worried, but she smiled kindly when she saw Effie.

'Stand, please,' the judge ordered then, and Effie stood with Zakari beside her, holding on to her elbow instead of her hand as the judge spoke in Arabic.

'Three times he will ask you if you want to be my wife,' Zakari translated. 'After the third time you will say yes…'

The words were delivered, then said three times.

'Yes!' Effie breathed.

The judge repeated the question to Zakari, though it was only cited once for him.

'Na'am.' Zakari nodded. 'Yes.'

Only then did the judge hand Effie the pen, and she signed the endless sheets of paper one by one as by her side Zakari did the same. Then they stood for what seemed like for ever as the Royal Seal was added to each one.

'Now what happens?' Effie whispered as the judge and aides sorted the papers.

'Now?' Zakari frowned.

'The private ceremony…'

'That was it,' Zakari said and Effie felt her heart still for a second. 'We are now officially married.'

CHAPTER SIX

His aides were anxious.

Zakari knew that.

In his pocket was the necklace his stepmother had given him to be worn by his bride on his wedding day. Right now he should be removing the Stefani stone from her neck and handing it to Hassan to place in the Calistan palace's vault, only his stepmother's words from yesteryear halted him.

'*Love the woman you give this to, Zakari, as your father loved me.*' He could hear Anya's rich voice as she had shown him her most sentimental jewels—the ones his father had had made for her a couple of years before they had both died. '*When everything is gone, Zakari, love is all we have. When the lights are dimmed at night, whether you sleep in a tent or a palace, it is she who you will hold in your arms.*'

He stared down at Effie, could see the tears welling in her eyes, could read the confusion on her face, sense the panic building in her. Zakari knew she was over-whelmed, and in this moment he could not do it to her—could not reveal the real reason she was here.

'Wait outside for me…' He gave her a brief kiss on

the cheek and waited till she was safely outside before he addressed his aides.

'I will get the necklace tonight.'

'But, Your Highness,' Hassan implored, 'you have waited so long for the Stefani jewel…'

'Then I can wait a little while longer. Go…' He would not be argued with, because he had no argument he could sensibly give. Of course he should claim the necklace now, except he couldn't. He wanted to speak to her properly, to tell her why the diamond was so important, why it had been imperative he marry her, but away from the cold eyes of his aides. So instead he dismissed them—Hassan, his aides, the judge, even his brother and Kalila. With one flick of his wrist he dismissed them all. 'I wish to be left alone. Tonight I am to be left undisturbed with my bride.'

His suite in the palace had been prepared for the wedding night.

Zakari dismissed both the maids waiting to prepare Effie for her night with her groom and the maids waiting to relieve him of the weight of his military uniform, choosing to take care of it himself. Unclipping the holster that held his sword, he took off the heavy, decorated jacket as Effie stood taking in the unfamiliar surrounds of Zakari's chambers, an area which, until now, she had never been permitted to enter, even as a maid.

It was a room that actually suited Zakari, Effie thought as she wandered around. The decor was more subdued than his tent, which had danced with colour. The floors had the same exquisite rugs, except they were darker, and heavy carved wooden furniture that held rare treasures lined the stone walls, which were softened only slightly with wall hangings. The centre-piece of the room was the bed. Large, high and impos-ing, it was draped in velvets of soft creams and browns and Effie couldn't comprehend that it was where she would now rest, that this very masculine room was where she would sleep.

For tonight, though, the room was softened only by hundreds of candles that twinkled on every available surface. A vast sunken bath had been filled, its surface laced with petals, and beyond that were French windows opening out onto a balcony that gazed towards the desert.

Effie wished she were there again now.

Wished she were back in the tent, where it was only they two. Wished that they had more time alone so she could get to know better the man who was now her husband.

A man who since she had woken in his arms this morning had been distant and aloof, her questions hanging in the air unanswered, and his eyes not meeting hers. A man she no longer recognised.

'What's behind here?' Effie stood at a heavy wooden door.

'Open it and see.'

'Oh!' Effie blinked as she did just that. 'It's where I was taken today.'

'That is your suite,' Zakari explained. 'You can dress there, bathe there. In the old days often couples slept apart—that is not my intention for us.'

Effie gave a small giggle, glad that was sorted; it wasn't her intention to sleep apart either.

'And that door?' Effie asked, crossing the large room and standing before an identical door.

'For the King's mistress…' Zakari smiled as Effie's heart stilled. 'Again, that goes back to days of old.'

'You won't keep a mistress?' Effie's voice was aghast. 'I could never…'

'Effie.' Finally he took her in his arms, understood how daunting this was for her, that the rituals and customs he had grown up with were alien to her. 'Why would I need a mistress?'

'I know…' She screwed her eyes closed and rested her head on his chest, glad to have him hold her again. 'I'm being silly. I guess in the old days it was all about duty, about convenience, whereas we love each other.'

He didn't answer. The musky incense was burning and filled every crevice of the room, yet it was her scent he craved and Zakari lowered his head into her hair. Despite her bulk as he held her in his arms, she felt so fragile and delicate that it seemed entirely natural to hold her trembling body and soothe her for a moment, before he told her.

Zakari could feel her heart fluttering in her throat as he caressed the back of her neck as, instead of telling her, he sought to reassure her.

'In thirty days,' Zakari explained, 'the palace will be ready—you shall have the wedding of your dreams.'

'It's not that,' Effie attempted. 'Today just seemed so cold, so formal.'

'Weddings are.'

'So lacking…'

'As I said, the public ceremony will be different.'

She didn't want different.

She wanted this. She wanted what they had away from the formalities that were so much a part of Zakari's existence.

Always tall, in his boots he was taller, stronger, the delicious masculine scent of him calming her as she breathed it in. She was his wife, that knowledge thrilled her—that Zakari was her husband melted her to her very core. It was that he was also Sheikh King Zakari Al'Farisi of Calista that Effie was having difficulty coming to terms with. But, here in his arms, away from the pomp and ceremony, when it was just they two, she felt her nerves disappear and actually felt safe.

'Let's eat,' Zakari said, leading her to the lavishly prepared low table, where Effie sat on one of the soft cushions, sipping on nectar-thick fruit juices and eyeing the goodies they would share.

A feast had been laid out for them.

The table had been laid with exquisitely prepared and presented delicacies and more traditional bridal fare: *mansaf*—a dish of rice and lamb, which Zakari explained should be eaten with the right hand, *argan*, which they had eaten on their first morning together, and for desert they ate *kanafeh*—finely shredded pastry noodles, filled with sweet cheese and sprinkled with pistachios. Even Zakari relaxed, feeding her slices of *halwah*, a traditional sweet confectionery, but, as lavish as the food was, to her surprise Effie struggled to eat. Food had always been her comfort, especially since her mother had died, but tonight she didn't need it. In the candlelight his features seemed softer, his smile so gentle, his laughter so ready, that Effie was able to be honest.

'I'm scared of letting everyone down,' she admitted. 'I don't understand all the customs, the rules…'

'I will teach you.'

'It's all been so fast.'

'So now we slow down…' Zakari smiled. 'Now the

people take some time to get used to the idea—my family, the Aristo royals—but we two, we are married—nothing can change that. No matter what happens.'

'What could happen?' Effie shivered at the ominous note in his voice.

'Nothing!' Zakari flashed a smile, only Effie didn't return it.

'I wish my mother was here...' Effie put down the *kanafeh*. 'She would have been so proud.'

'I'm sure she would have been,' Zakari agreed.

'What about you? You must miss your father on a day like today.'

Zakari gave a tight shrug.

'And Anya too?'

'Of course...' Zakari breathed, making a mental note to correct her tomorrow; she should not ask such things, should not touch on such subjects with him.

Her blue eyes dazzled like jewels, her sweet mouth relaxing in his company, more trusting now they were alone.

'Your other brothers—will they be at the ceremony?'

'Of course.'

'Aarif seems happy.'

'He is,' Zakari agreed, then unbended slightly. It was his wedding night, he told himself, he was entitled to relax and talk. 'He never was happy, till he met Kalila. His guilt over what happened to Zafir was too great. Now, though, he is finally moving on, doing things for himself.'

'As he should.' Effie smiled. 'As should you.'

'I have more responsibility than Aarif.' Suddenly Zakari was guarded. 'Sometimes I have to do things that perhaps, if I were not King, I would not choose to...'

'Such as?' The Stefani diamond was gleaming between her breasts, her eyes so trusting as they smiled over to him, and Zakari actually felt a sweat break on his brow as he worked up to telling her.

'My people have to come first—their future, their well-being is in my hands. At times I have to make difficult choices.

'You are happy?' Zakari suddenly checked. 'With how things have worked out?'

'I never imagined I could be so happy.' Effie smiled.

'You will have help with your wardrobe, jewels, anything you want—and if you want to change some of the rooms to your taste…'

'That's not why I'm happy!' Effie scolded. 'The title, the jewels…' She shook her head. 'Zakari, I would be happy if we lived in a tent, a tiny little tent in the middle of a field, so long as we have each other.'

The words were so close to what Anya had said, for a second Zakari closed his eyes. Her enthusiasm, her devotion, both warmed and chilled him, because here was the first woman he had ever met who did not seem to care for his title, a woman who seemed only to care for him. But now they were safely married, surely she could drop the act a touch and relish her new status, or at least acknowledge how wonderful her new-found riches were, yet she truly didn't seem to care and it chilled him because now he must tell her…

'To tell you the truth,' Effie continued happily as Zakari's head tightened, 'I'm terrified. I have no desire to be Sheikha Stefania and all that it will entail, but so long as I have you…' there was an urgent note to her voice '…knowing I have your love, I can put up with anything. I will do my very best to make you proud.'

'You will.' Zakari's voice was gruff. 'You do. Effie, I need to…' He started as they both spoke together.

'I would love a bath…' She let out a long, exhausted sigh. 'Sorry, you were saying? You need to…?'

'Nothing.' Zakari shook his head. 'It will keep.' He gestured to the vast sunken bath. 'Have your bath. You deserve to relax after today.'

'It will be cold by now!' Effie walked over, ready to drain it, blinking that it was still deliciously warm…

'It stays hot for as long as you want it…'

'Like you…' Effie flushed at her provocative words. Zakari just stared at her and there was this moment, this tiny moment where she wavered; to undress, to just stand naked before him, was so very terrifying, yet he loved her, Effie reminded herself. This man who could have anyone had chosen her, considered her beautiful. She didn't want to disappoint him now by becoming retiring and shy. Tonight she wanted to be for him the woman she was slowly becoming.

And so she undressed.

She slipped off her dress and underwear as Zakari watched, then slid into the warmth of the water, ducking her head under and feeling the lacquer in her hair dissolve.

And Zakari watched.

Watched her glorious body glisten with oil and water and as she surfaced saw her hair hang in dark waves.

Tomorrow, Zakari decided, his throat suddenly dry, he would tell her tomorrow.

Why spoil things tonight?

For the first time he removed his own boots, gazing at her in the soapy water, her eyes inviting him to join her, and Zakari undressed quickly. As he slid into the warm soapy water her warm wet body slipped into his and her hungry mouth greeted him and Zakari could only marvel at the woman he had unleashed. His hands massaged her soapy breasts, her legs coiled around his waist and she giggled as they slipped slightly, his head dunking under the water as Effie's did the same, and as they rose to the surface she laughed and so too did Zakari.

Laughed as he never, ever had.

And for the first time he understood Aarif's words. For the very first time he glimpsed a future where, no matter the strains and stresses of the day, no matter the weight and burdens of the Kingdom of Adamas, he could come home to this, to love and laughter and passion, to just be himself.

To just *be*.

He could deal with any challenges thrown at him, if he had those precious hours at night, with Effie.

As her hands soaped his chest and slippery fingers worked down and massaged his impressive erection; as he explored her body, made weightless by waters, the faint steam rising around, Zakari truly learnt how to relax, how to switch off from a world that constantly made demands, how to just let go and enjoy.

She was *so* enjoyable.

Despite the sumptuous heat of the room, Effie shivered from too long in the bath when they finally came out, and he wrapped her in a thick towel, then laid her on the bed and proceeded to slowly dry every shivering inch of her skin, till she was soft and pliant and warm. Then he lay beside her, talking to her between kisses, getting to know his beautiful bride and hoping to ward off the morning.

She tasted of soap, and felt divine. Her hair was still

damp and it lay wet and heavy on his chest as her tongue kissed its way down as her soft warm hand crept up his thighs and then held him in her palm.

'Do you remember how you kissed me there…?'

'Of course.' He grew in her hand at the memory.

'If I were to kiss you—in the same way…' Effie faltered, unsure if she might offend, unsure if she even knew what to do '…would it be as nice?'

'It would be…' Zakari caught his breath, could not continue to speak as she did just that, her pretty smiling mouth kissing his length *so* inexpertly, yet it felt divine. Hot, chaste kisses that had him drag in his breath as they reached his tip, her tongue swirling in a way that had his heart still in his chest.

'Is like this okay?'

'It is…' Zakari couldn't complete his sentence as she kissed him more thoroughly.

Just as she had at first tentatively kissed his mouth and had then grown hungry for more, Effie kissed him ever deeper, her tongue circling, her body greedy for his.

And then, checking his pleasure, for a second she stilled, her blue eyes glittered up at him as her soft pink mouth still held him and Zakari's fingers knotted in her hair as she set back to work. And for the first time in his life, Zakari relaxed, just relaxed and enjoyed, because he knew she was enjoying it too; because with Effie there was no rush, no benchmark to match, just this mutual pleasure that was beyond anything he had ever experienced.

The soft swell of her intimate place pressing into his thigh had him pushing his leg up to massage, his free hand searching to pleasure her, not to impress, but because he wanted to, and feeling her sweet, slippery warmth, feeling her pleasure, he wanted to slip under the surface and let go, to accept the release she offered, only he couldn't…

The Stefani diamond was heavy against his thigh as her tongue worked its magic. The reason it was still around her neck was so that they might consummate the marriage.

Duty must prevail.

'Come here.'

He dragged her up to him.

He cupped her buttocks as he held her over his straining length and found that duty could also mean pleasure as he watched her sweet, intimate butterfly lips cloak him, hold him and caress him.

His eyes were on a different prize as they climaxed together—the Stefani diamond forgotten as he stared up at her face, watching it contort in ecstasy as he shuddered into her. He held her after till she was spent, till the last flutters of her orgasm stroked him as he nestled deep within her. Only when she lay on her side, when he spooned into her, one hand gently cupping her breast as they drifted off to sleep, did he remember, the Stefani stone slipping down the chain and silently coming to rest on the back of his hand.

The marriage was consummated, Zakari realised.

There was no reason not to tell her.

Except one—surely it could wait till morning.

CHAPTER SEVEN

IT WAS his duty, Zakari reminded himself. He had to secure the diamond and to do so he'd had to consummate the marriage.

Hadn't he?

Not for the first time since waking had he questioned last night's motives, yet for the first time he could not shrug off his thoughts. The sun would be rising in a matter of minutes, shedding light on the day ahead, demanding he deal with things. But how could he tell her now?

Should he have told her the truth in the desert?

For the first time in his life, Zakari's conscience was pricking. Effie would not have dared argue with a king—she would not have denied him the stone. And even if she had married him out of duty, or on the chance she was carrying his heir, she had given her heart to him before the wedding—last night had not been necessary.

Yet it had!

He had wanted her, had wanted that perfect night with her before he told her the truth.

'Zakari?' She came up behind him on the royal balcony, her hand on his taut shoulder, her warm lips kissing the taut flesh of his back as he gazed out to the pre-dawn desert.

'Come back to bed...' Effie reasoned. 'Zakari, it is too cool here.'

How much easier would it be to take her back to bed, to make love? He could feel himself harden as her warm lips nuzzled his shoulders, wanted to deny the dawn and prolong their time.

Yet already things were in place. Today she would find out, whether he told her or not.

There was a line of orange on the far horizon, saffron fingers slowly fanning out, a screech from above as the birds awoke and he looked upwards as a dark shadow soared.

Zakari had never liked falconry.

A sport amongst his people, it had never appealed to him. Oh, he had partaken at times when it was necessary, and yet watching that beautiful beast circling its prey, watching it soar so high as the tiny vermin continued unawares, he had, as a child, shuddered at what lay ahead. Even as a teenager, though he had grinned to his father, still an unseen part of him had shuddered as the bird had swooped, nausea had risen as the bird had returned to his leathered arm with its bloody beak bearing its gift.

He felt like a falcon now.

Circling his unwitting prey.

His little silver bird smiled innocently as he turned around to face her—to face the truth.

'There is something you must know. Today there will be an announcement.'

'About us?' Effie checked.

'That was released yesterday,' Zakari explained.

'Today the news will break that the missing half of the Stefani diamond has been found…'

Effie's eyes were wide. 'It was lost?'

'It was replaced with a fake and both palaces have kept it quiet, but the fact was Prince Alex's coronation could not go ahead without the missing half of the Stefani diamond.'

'So it can go ahead now?'

'No.' Zakari shook his head. 'The stones are to be reunited. King Christos's Legacy is about to be fulfilled.'

'I don't understand.'

'I am in possession of the missing half of the Stefani jewel.' Zakari's voice was thick, his eyes not meeting hers. 'Which means that I will now rule both Calista and Aristo.'

'You…' Effie blinked, a smile breaking on her face, as dazzling and as stunning and as delightful as the rapidly rising sun. She offered him her heartfelt congratulations. 'Zakari, I am so proud for you, I'll do everything I can to support you…'

With every word she made it harder, her trust, her faith in him, so absolute it would take an axe to shatter it. 'When did this happen?' Effie continued. 'When was it found?'

Turning, he fingered the necklace that hung between her pearly white breasts and with his heart in his mouth he raised the axe to fell her.

'This…' Zakari cleared his throat '…is the Stefani diamond.' He saw her frown. 'This is the missing half of the Stefani diamond.'

'Don't be silly.' Effie smiled, the only woman who might say that to a king and get away with it. 'I already told you, it was my mother's necklace. It is worth nothing… It's probably just made of glass.'

'No.' Zakari shook his head. 'That is the jewel I have been searching for—I would recognise it anywhere.'

'Why would my mother have such a precious diamond?' Effie reasoned. 'She was a palace maid…' He watched the soft smile slip from her lips, a smudge of a frown darken her pretty features. 'My mother wasn't a thief.'

'A thief could not take this. These are royal jewels, guarded, accessible only to the highest members of the family.'

'Then how?' Effie blinked.

'Your mother,' Zakari said slowly, 'was King Aegeus's mistress.'

'My mother?' Effie shook her head at the impossibility. 'Zakari, that is impossible. How could you even think it?'

'The pool at Kionia…' Zakari interrupted.

'What about it?'

'Queen Tia commissioned it.' Zakari's voice was so deep and low, hoarse almost, that she had to strain her ears to hear it. 'The year Princess Elissa was born— long after your mother worked there.'

'That doesn't mean anything…' She didn't want to get it, didn't want to understand what he was trying to explain to her. Instead Effie wanted to go back to bed where it was warm, wanted her king, her man to make love to her as he had last night, wanted him to love her as she had been so sure he had.

'For your mother to have seen it, for your mother to even know about it…' Zakari pushed, but Effie was refusing to hear him.

'Maybe she went back…' Effie attempted. 'Perhaps she did some casual work…'

'There are no casual staff at Kionia.'

'Maybe she just read about it,' Effie begged. 'Heard about it from someone…'

'Your mother was Aegeus's lover…' His lips sneered around the name—the man he hated most in the world. 'He gave her many jewels, some of which she sold over the years. I have returned them to their rightful place, but the only one she kept was the Stefani stone. He set her up in the cottage—palace maids don't buy cottages. Aegeus was the one who kept her.'

'No.' Still she denied it. 'Not my mother and Aegeus!'

'Yes Aegeus…' Zakari spat—he wasn't finding this easy, his anger at himself and at Aegeus turning on her. 'Your name!' he flared. 'Your real name is Stefania. You cannot deny what is on your birth certificate—you were named after the jewel he gave to her. Your mother was his whore—'

'My mother was no whore…' She slapped his cheek, then when it didn't help she slapped it again. 'If she is a whore, then what does that make me?'

'You are my wife.'

'I wasn't when we first slept together.'

'You are my wife now.'

'Why?' she challenged. 'Because you love me, because you want me…or because of this…' She saw it then—the change she had seen, the breath that had caught in his throat when she had dressed for him, the wonder in his eyes hadn't been for her, hadn't been at her beauty, but at the power he had glimpsed.

'You, Zakari, are the whore.' She ripped off the necklace and hurled it at him. 'You are the one who slept with me for gain! Well, take it!'

It hurt like hell to take off her mother's jewel, but it was also impossible to keep. It was a thing—a possession, not hers to hold on to, just as she was a possession, a thing, a means to an end.

'Where are you going?' As Effie ran inside the suite he watched as she rapidly dressed.

'Home.'

'Home? Your home is here with me. You are my wife…' He grabbed her wrist and furiously she tried to shake him off, only she couldn't. Her unshod foot was her only method of attack and she kicked him in the shin, hurting herself more than him no doubt, but the shock was enough for Zakari to loosen his grip.

Not the shock of any pain she had inflicted.

More the anger in her.

The hurt.

And strangest of all…more than a flicker of guilt.

Well, what did she expect? Zakari reasoned, pacing the bedroom after she had gone. Kings didn't fall in love with maids. She should be pleased; in time she would be pleased… She had status now, a title, she had more than she could ever have dreamed of in her meagre existence.

Picking up the phone, he summoned Hassan to his suite, handing over the treasure and telling him to break the news to the Aristo palace and also to the press that the diamond was now his.

That Christos's Legacy was about to be fulfilled!

'Your Highness!' Hassan held the jewel in his palm more tenderly than if it were a child. 'You have waited for this moment for so long.'

'Where is Sheikha Stefania?' Zakari asked.

'She asked to be taken to her mother's home.' Hassan

gave an exaggerated sigh. 'She will calm down, she will return soon…'

Only Zakari wasn't so sure. When he had signed the marriage documents he had expected hurt, anger even, when he eventually told her the news. But the woman who piece by piece had revealed herself last night was a woman he hadn't bargained on. She had blossomed before his eyes and under the guise of his love she had flourished, and this morning he had watched her heart shatter.

'I want a car placed outside the house,' Zakari instructed. 'The guard is to make sure she is not disturbed and that she does not speak with the press. When she is ready to return to the palace he will bring her to me.'

The news that Zakari had the stone ripped through the kingdoms of Aristo and Calista. Even Zakari was slightly taken aback by the fallout as he watched the breaking news on television. Regular programming had been suspended and on every channel it was the only subject on people's minds. There was wailing in the streets of Aristo, while the Calistan people, rather than celebrating, were to Zakari's surprise rather stunned and subdued. The Aristan royals had offered no comment but senior aides had already been despatched to Calista and were demanding to sight the stone and prove its authenticity. Second, third, fourth editions of the newspapers were being released, the later editions hazarding rapid guesses at what would happen now— how the transition of power might take place and the daunting tasks that lay ahead.

Only the Calistan royals, it seemed, were in the mood for celebration.

Zakari, naturally the head of the table, joined by his

brothers and sisters and Aarif's and Kaliq's wives. Effie was noticeable only by her absence.

'She will soon come to accept it,' Aarif said.

'Of course she will,' Kalila agreed with her husband. 'She has royal blood in her, after all.'

Zakari's lips were suddenly dry. Reaching for his drink, he sipped the juice, but it did nothing to quench his thirst, and he gestured impatiently for his water to be replenished before taking a long sip, only it did nothing to refresh him either.

The bastard of Aegeus she might be, but there was more royal blood in Effie's veins than his own and he had witnessed it first-hand that very morning—that fire, pride and indefinable strength that marked her out as being royal. It was the very thing that Zakari had worked hard to master from scratch, but Effie had been born to it.

'Would you like me to talk to her?' Eleni, Kaliq's new wife, offered. She had been a lowly stable girl herself before Kaliq had swept her off her feet and knew some of how Effie must be feeling. 'I know how hard it is to adjust. Maybe if she had a friend…'

'I will talk to her!' Zakari rejected Eleni's offer with a terse response. 'Tomorrow she will return to the palace.'

Eleni still hadn't quite mastered the basics of dining with a king and her pursed lips and slight eye-roll let everyone at the table know what she thought. The only saving grace, Kaliq told her later, trying himself not to laugh at his fiery wife's ways, was that Zakari had been too distracted to notice.

Lying in bed that night Zakari missed Effie.

Not just the lovemaking, but the ease, the laughter, the comfort she brought to the room.

Tomorrow he would get her; Zakari's mind was made up.

Tomorrow he would tell her to stop this nonsense and to take her rightful place by his side.

CHAPTER EIGHT

HER mother's things, her mother's home, *her* home, had always brought her comfort.

But not today.

Wandering amongst familiar things, Effie longed for the ignorance of yesterday.

She stared into her mother's empty jewel box, remembering as a child how she'd tried on her pretty things—the necklaces she'd draped around her neck, the rings she'd placed on her little fat fingers.

Royal jewels! Effie cringed now at the innocent memory. She had been playing with royal jewels—jewels her mother had sold over the years in an effort to support them.

Every part of her felt tainted.

What a fool. Effie sat on the threadbare sofa and huddled into the corner and stared at the rich oil paintings and books that lined the walls. What a fool she had been to never question her mother, what a blind stupid fool to believe that her mother could have supported them both on a palace maid's savings.

From where she sat she could see the expensive cream car parked on the dust road, the tinted windows shielding the occupant, but occasionally the window wound down and a cigarette was flicked out, revealing a burly occupant wearing dark glasses who made Effie shiver.

She was a prisoner in her own home.

Hungry for information, for answers, she dragged a ladder from the shed outside and into the cramped hall and climbed up to the loft. With utter disregard for her safety, she dragged out box after box and threw them to the floor beneath her. The task of going through her mother's things, her photos, her letters, had been too painful to comprehend, yet it was imperative to Effie that she do it now.

Sitting on the hall floor, she truly didn't know where to start, her hand reaching for the first box, pulling out a random letter, and the second she opened it every fear was confirmed, every dream broken, just as she had deep down known it would be.

Zakari wouldn't have got this wrong.

May 19th 1985
Lydia,

Again, I waited for you last night, just as I did last year. You know it is too dangerous for me to come to you. I am pleading with you to come to me, to contact me, to let me know that you are well.

I know we cannot be together, but we promised to meet once a year. Please don't deny us that one pleasure.

Till next year
Yours always
Ax

She would have been one year old, Effie realised, tears coursing down her cheeks, and the year before that her mother would have been pregnant with her—no wonder she hadn't dared meet him.

She read a few more. Each letter, each passing year Aegeus's pleas were more desperate, more urgent, then suddenly the letters stopped. Aegeus had clearly given in.

With a weary eye, Effie stared at the boxes, but couldn't face them now. She had started reading at the end of their story, but was just too exhausted, too drained, to start from the beginning.

There would be time for that later, Effie knew, watching her front door darken and realising her small respite was over.

Zakari had come to claim her.

'You will come back!' Zakari stood imposing and huge and just completely out of place in the tiny modest lounge. 'You have no choice but to come back.'

'There's a clause in the marriage for divorce!' Effie couldn't even bring herself to look at him. 'I read it myself!'

He paced like a caged lion, stopping every now and then and staring at the photos, the pictures that lined the walls, pulling down books from the shelves.

'These are first editions!' He shook his head. 'This picture alone would equal the value of your home—yet you were working as a maid.'

'I didn't know.' Effie shivered in her own misery. 'They've just always been there. I was hardly going to assume they were gifts from a king.'

He was so invasive, just so consumed with his own self-righteousness, he didn't think twice about striding into her mother's room and throwing scorn on her things.

'These jewel boxes are from Egypt!' Zakari shook his head in disbelief. 'These would have been gifts from the Egyptian royals to the Aristan palace…' He picked up the tiny glass perfume bottles Effie had once cherished and her misery deepened as each precious memory was tarnished. 'These are part of a rare collection. Your home is furnished by the Aristan palace!' Zakari sneered. 'You have no need to worry about not fitting in—you have been surrounded by rare treasures all your life!'

'I didn't know!' Effie sobbed.

'Whether you like it or not,' Zakari said, only slightly more gently now, 'things have changed. It is impossible for you to go back to your old life. People know now who your father was. It will be impossible for you to work, to carry on as before…' He watched the tears that rolled down her cheeks, felt a strange twist of guilt for what he had put her through, then righted himself— what choice had he had? And anyway, he had rescued her. She was nothing but a lowly palace maid when he met her, now she would wear the finest clothes, walk with kings—so why was she crying?

'You have a duty to the people.'

'What duty?'

'How will it help the people of Aristo and Calista to hear their king is divorced? There is already enough turmoil without a marriage crisis looming. You will return with me now. You will serve the people I now rule.'

'You have what you want,' Effie pleaded. 'Why do you still need me?'

'Because kings do not divorce!' Zakari roared. 'Their wives do not walk out on them after just one night of marriage—and you shall not walk out on me. You will remain by my side.'

She knew when she was beaten, knew he was right—however much she might want to return, her old life didn't exist any more.

'I will walk by your side... I will eat at your table...' despite her tears, Effie's voice was strong '...but never, ever again will my heart be by your side.'

He didn't understand what she was saying—she had agreed to his rules, would stay in the palace, there would be no scandal of divorce... Everything he wanted he had...except one thing.

'Arrange another room for me.'

'No. You will sleep in my bed.'

'Never...' Effie spat as if the mere thought repulsed her. 'You can take your mistress if tradition is so important to you, then go back to the ways of old, Zakari. There's already a room waiting for her!'

'We need heirs.'

How basic, how sad that it all came down to this.

'I will come to you when I am fertile.' Effie's voice was flat and utterly void of emotion as she delivered the cold facts. 'You can take me then.'

'Take you?'

'Do your business,' Effie said. 'That is all you get from me.'

This wasn't going as planned. He had expected her to be upset, angry even, but she was beyond angry now. Her eyes, when they met his, were cold and hard, that pretty mouth that had smiled and chatted so readily with him, just this tight line now.

'You are upset,' Zakari conceded. 'I accept that, but in time you will see that there was no other way.'

'You could have spoken to me about the jewel. You could have told me you needed it.'

'You really expect that I would discuss royal business with a maid?' Zakari frowned. 'Until you were my wife there was nothing that could be discussed.'

'Well, you got what you wanted,' Effie responded.

'Fine,' Zakari clipped, but the last word would be his. 'You can sleep alone until the official wedding ceremony takes place—the palace staff will accept that, and you will have time to get used to your new position. But after that,' Zakari stated, 'you will be my wife, in every sense of the word.'

CHAPTER NINE

SHE had never felt lonelier.

Surrounded by people, every minute of her day planned and accounted for, never had Effie felt more alone.

She was awoken early, her dresser and make-up artist arriving together. Her face was made up, her clothes chosen for her and her hair brushed and coiled severely, till she was deemed suitable to have breakfast with the King.

Oh, she could see his bored eyes greet her in the morning, knew she disappointed on so many levels, but then he had disappointed her.

She was a mere shadow of her former self. With every diction lesson, with every hour she had to sit through and listen to the history of Calista, or be versed in politics, with every degrading minute spent being shown how to walk, how to sit, how to exit from a car, how to accept a handshake or a curtsy, Effie felt as if she were being eroded.

And now, after three weeks of training, she was apparently ready to be unleashed to the hungry public.

A charity polo match was being held on Calista, one that would raise vast sums of money for the orphanage.

A noble cause for a noble game, Zakari explained in a clipped tone as he read all the morning papers—something he did each morning as she sipped her sweet coffee.

Aarif was joining his brothers and taking part in an official polo match for the first time, which was enough on its own to pull an impressive crowd, but with the royal wedding just over a week away the people of Calista were frantic for a glimpse of the woman who would be their beloved King's bride and every expensive seat had long since been sold.

'You are nervous?' Zakari checked, his face tightening when instead of answering him she just nodded. 'Kalila and Eleni will be with you, they will guide you and as soon as the match is over I will join you.' It irritated him that his attempt at reassurance clearly didn't work, that the conversation that had once flowed so easily between them was still so stilted and forced. 'You have your wardrobe chosen; your hair and make-up will be done. There is nothing to be nervous about.'

'I'd rather choose my own clothes.' Effie gulped. 'They don't seem to know what suits me.'

'You have the finest dressmaker in Calista,' Zakari retorted, his gaze inadvertently falling to the pastry in her fingers, and Effie burned in one blush, hating that she wasn't svelte, hating every humiliating fitting for her wedding dress. 'She was the Queen's top designer.'

'But she doesn't listen to me…' Effie attempted, then gave in. How could Zakari possibly understand her struggle? The dressmakers and make-up artists had been like gods to Effie and she had made their beds and cleaned their rooms. Even though no one had ever uttered a word, even though all the palace staff were polite, she could feel their mocking eyes on her, could feel their hostility—that they now had to wait on the lowest of maids. 'The maids don't respect me.'

'Then you have to assert yourself,' Zakari clipped. 'They are here to wait on you…expect it and it will happen.' Oh, he made it sound so easy. 'You will look fine.'

'Of course.' Effie nodded, blinking back the tears in her eyes at his inadvertent choice of word. With the best dressmaker, the best make-up artist and *everything* at her disposal, that all he could summon to describe her was *fine* rammed home her unsuitability for the role she had been thrust into.

'I have to go now.' He stood to leave. 'Noor…' he snapped his fingers at a maid '…remove the newspapers.'

'Leave the newspapers, Noor,' Effie said, and then met his eyes. 'You said I should assert myself.'

'Why do you insist on reading them?' Zakari said with a weary sigh.

'You read them,' Effie pointed out.

'I have to keep abreast of all the goings-on. I have to gauge people's reactions to the news that I will soon be King of Aristo.'

'If you don't leave them I will walk to the shop and buy them for myself. Which will really give them something to write about!'

'Fine!' Zakari shrugged. 'If you insist. I will see you after the match.'

As the door was opened for him Zakari turned, just in time to see her reach for another pastry, her misery palpable.

'Try to enjoy today… It is for a good cause. A lot of money is being raised for the orphanage on Calista.' She said nothing, her hand just frozen over the pastry. 'It is an exciting game too—and that Aarif is playing makes it especially important to me.'

'I'm sure it will be wonderful,' she dutifully replied, only it wasn't enough. He could hear Kalila laughing in the palace corridors as she walked to the entrance with her husband, to no doubt kiss him goodbye, and he wanted the same from Effie.

'Are you going to wish me luck?' Zakari demanded.

'You don't need luck, Zakari,' Effie answered dully. 'If you set your mind to something, you get it.' She gave a pale smile. 'I'm sure it will be the same today.'

There was no escape from her humiliation.

Picking up the newspapers Zakari himself had just read, she read of her very public shame.

Oh, the Calistan papers were discreet—more joyous of the news that their king would now rule both islands than focussing on the methods.

The Aristan newspapers, though, were savage.

Pointing out how power-hungry Zakari was—and the lengths he would go to. That when he could have had any woman he wanted, he would marry a fat, illegitimate maid if it meant he would rule both islands.

Zakari had merely shrugged when she had at first wept over them, and explained that when the transition of power was complete they would not dare to print such things, but that just hurt Effie more—that he had said *things*, instead of *lies*.

They were especially brutal this morning.

A particularly scathing piece, in one of the trashier papers, even questioned the legality of the marriage, as to how Zakari could even bring himself to consummate it!

An appalling caricature of them both followed on the

next page, Zakari, dressed in his military uniform, but with a peg on his nose as he lowered his head to kiss her.

They'd made her look like a pig.

And now she had to face them.

Had to somehow stand proud, knowing what people had read this morning.

Effie closed her eyes and wept.

Anya's top designer she might have been, but Queen Anya had been sixty when she had died and she, Effie, was only twenty-five.

Queen Anya had been tall and elegant, whereas she, Effie, was short and overweight.

Anya had also died five years ago, Effie gulped, standing with the other royals as they waited to make their entrance. She had been dressed in a pale pink satin suit, a floor-length skirt and a fitted jacket with extravagant beading and embroidery that was so long it covered her bottom, but it made her legs look short.

Five years, Effie realised as she nervously glanced at her new family, all effortless in their elegance, was a long time in fashion.

As the announcement was made they entered the royal box and the whole stadium stood to attention, for a moment all heads lowered in reverence, but that reprieve was fleeting. The formalities over, Effie felt every eye in the crowd fix on her, assessing her, taking in every uncomfortable detail as Zakari's choice for a bride was closely scrutinised and, Effie realised as the cameras started flashing, photographed.

Effie had always lived life in the shadows, and happily so, and it was excruciating to sit and listen to the hum of the crowd, knowing, just knowing they were talking about her.

'They will soon get used to you,' Kalila said kindly. 'For now, of course, there is a lot of interest.' She gave a kind smile. 'You will get used to it too.'

Oh, she doubted it. Sitting beside the woman who had initially been chosen as a suitable bride for her husband, more and more Effie realised just how very unsuitable she herself was.

Kalila was so naturally elegant; her conversation with the other dignitaries was polite and engaging. Effie knew Zakari was delighted for his brother and that he wasn't remotely jealous of the union that had taken place with his once-chosen bride, but it unsettled Effie, who now saw up close what was expected of Zakari's wife. She knew she failed miserably.

'Are you looking forward to the wedding?' Kalila checked as the game neared its conclusion. They were in the final *chukka*, Eleni had explained, and Effie was willing the match to be over so she could escape. The scores were even and the mounting excitement of the crowd meant at least they were too occupied to stare at her! 'Or is that a silly question? I remember how nervous I was on my wedding...' She trailed off, remembering, perhaps, that she had been intended for Zakari. 'Tell me about your dress,' she asked instead. 'I am sure it is stunning.'

'It is very...' Effie struggled to make a positive description. There was not a single thing about her dress she liked. Her tiny murmurs of protests had been waved away or ignored by the designers as they had continued to stick her with pins. 'Elaborate!'

'Tell me about it.' Eleni, who was sitting on the other

side of Effie, was slightly less intimidating, but even if she had once been a commoner she was so feisty and confident in her own skin and so knowledgeable of the game, Effie felt drab in comparison. 'It is so hard at first.' She gave a sympathetic smile. 'I remember how I struggled with my wardrobe, but Kaliq suggested I try designers from Aristo…'

Yes, Effie thought bitterly, but Kaliq loves you.

Oh, Eleni was kind, and she tried to include her in conversation, but she kept getting diverted, watching her husband and the unfolding last minutes of the game with undisguised glee.

'Too fast!' Eleni was on the edge of her seat, then, remembering her place, sat back, but Effie could feel her tension, and looking onto the pitch she saw the reason for it.

Zakari was thundering down the emerald pitch, the end of the match just a minute or so away, and, as Eleni had explained, another goal and Zakari's team would win, but, even to Effie's inexperienced eye, she knew Zakari was going way too fast. He was almost out of his saddle as he swooped to hit the ball and Effie could feel her stomach in her mouth, sure he wouldn't stop in time, biting down on her lip as he raised his mallet then connected with the ball, thrusting it and scoring what was surely the winning goal, then saluting the air with his fist as his team congratulated him and the crowd went wild…

As Zakari did it again!

Glancing upwards to the royal box, Zakari saw Eleni was applauding loudly until she remembered to contain herself a touch, and Kalila was smiling demurely, yet on the face of his bride, instead of pride and admiration, all he could see was her pale taut features. He didn't recognise it as fear.

Did nothing make her smile? Zakari thought savagely.

Did nothing he did make her proud?

He'd nearly broken his neck going for that ball! Yes, he'd been showing off a bit perhaps, but, hell, did nothing impress her?

He could have any woman he wanted in this crowd. Kicking his horse angrily, Zakari turned it on thigh power alone and sped off, the whole stadium on their feet in adulation, yet the one woman who could have him, the one woman whom, he reluctantly admitted to himself, he had been hoping to impress, just looked pained and bored.

'Excellent work, Your Highness.'

Tanya, a pretty stable girl, took the reins as Zakari slipped off his horse. Despite the punishing heat and exertion of the game, he had barely worked up a sweat, but his muscles pumped and his veins were thrumming with the testosterone of victory. He could see Tanya's breasts jutting high in her T-shirt, see that before she lowered her eyes she held his gaze for just a second too long... His groin was on fire, and on any other occasion he would have indulged in a flirt, hell, might have taken her between showering and changing...

Only he didn't want to.

Accepting congratulations, smiling as his back was slapped, Zakari scanned the hungry crowd with restless eyes. Only the elite were allowed in this area and he watched them part as his wife made her way over, nervous, plain, overweight, and in the most terrible suit. His heart suddenly went out to her as he realised how humiliating, how daunting today must have been for her, and he wished she would let him support her. He was furious with the newspapers, enraged and disgusted, and more than a touch embarrassed too…

Embarrassed that they considered the King might sleep with a pig, when she was actually the most beautiful of them all. He knew it was only himself that could see it, *had* seen it, had seen her very real beauty, that pale face flushed with arousal, that taut mouth parted in pleasure as she had sobbed out his name. That heat was stirring in his groin again. All the nights she had denied him were nearing an end now. In just over a week he would have her again lying in his arms, and she would be beautiful again, the way she had once been for him.

'C-congratulations…' Effie stammered, hating that all eyes were on her, knowing they were watching how they interacted, positive that everyone was laughing at her, that Zakari was ashamed. Then suddenly he did the strangest thing: Zakari, breaking with protocol, pulled her towards him, his mouth hard on hers. It was the briefest of kisses, but it felt as if he were branding her, claiming her, showing them all that she was his. Effie could feel his erection pressing into her, the heady scent of him filling her nostrils, and for a small second her defences were down. The bliss of his hot mouth, the feel of him pressed against her were like a match meeting gas—she flared. Caught off guard, for just a moment she responded to his kiss, then she checked herself. Zakari could attempt as many public displays of affection as he wanted, but she refused to play for the cameras when the truth was, in private, they were apart.

'Did you enjoy it?' He was still holding her, black eyes boring into her.

'I didn't understand much of it.'

'It was your first time.' Zakari's mouth curled into a smile. 'The first few times are often confusing, but you will get a taste for it.' His groin was pressed into hers, his message clear. 'You *will* adore it…'

He released her then, the crowd swarming to congratulate him. Eleni, though, was having trouble trying to concentrate on what her husband was saying… Zakari's wife had been lovely to talk to, a real sweetheart actually, but clearly, Eleni had thought, she was out of her depth, and from what Kaliq had told her there was no love lost between the two of them…

Or so she had thought…

The way Zakari had charged towards her reminded Eleni of a stallion being let out of his box, but most curious of all was how Effie had responded, like a nervous mare, yet, Eleni could have sworn, for a moment she had been aroused all the same…

Kalila was having trouble working it out too.

Later that night, as she was lying in her husband's arms, her mind wandered to the polo match again.

'Your brother's new wife,' Kalila started, 'she struggled today—'

'She will learn in time,' Aarif interrupted. 'It must be hard adjusting to a role she was not born for, especially knowing that all he wanted from her was the stone.'

'He wants more than the stone.' Kalila smiled into the darkness. 'I think Sheikha Stefania might just surprise us all. Your brother is smitten.'

'Zakari?' Aarif laughed. 'He is not smitten. The only thing my brother craves is power.'

'I'm not so sure…' Kalila differed as further along the walls of the palace Zakari wrestled with the same.

He had everything.

Everything he had prayed for.

All the power he had ever dreamed of.

Yet all he felt was empty.

Her lips had tasted so sweet this afternoon, and he *had* felt her relent for a second, and a little of what he craved had left him hungry for more. For the first time he broke his promise and, restless, aroused, he walked through his room to the adjoining door, a curse on his lips when he realised she had locked it. He was tempted to knock, to demand that she join him, but he halted himself.

Kings did not beg!

In one week, she would come to him!

CHAPTER TEN

FOR a royal wedding, it was a somewhat subdued affair.

Oh, the crowds turned out and duly cheered. The ceremony was full of all the pomp and grandeur that would be expected for the wedding of a king, only with every photo, every introduction, every curtsy, Effie was humiliated more.

The brief civil ceremony had been her wedding and that one blissful night afterwards had been her honeymoon.

This was a sham.

But then, Effie reflected, so had been her first wedding!

After the ceremony, after the endless speeches and photo calls, the maidens had undressed and then bathed her, taking down her stiff hair and brushing it, but the curls and soft hairbrush and mass of lacquer had just made it fluff, and Effie was so sick of it she had dismissed them, preferring to prepare for her night with Zakari alone. As if she were dressing for the gallows, she pulled on the white silk nightdress that had been laid out for her, the French lace straining over her bosoms as finally she opened the door that adjoined their rooms.

The maids had been busy here too, the room just as

it had been on their first wedding night was scented and lit with candles, a deep bath drawn and the sheets turned back. Every detail had been attended to, Effie realised, as for the first time in the thirty days since she had signed the papers Zakari insisted that she now join him in his bed.

'Here…' He handed her a glass of icy champagne, perhaps to relax her, but all it did was make her remember the first and last time she had tasted champagne, when she had mistaken the glint of want in his eyes, when she had foolishly believed that it was aimed at her.

'Effie, we are married now, in every sense of the word.'

'I know that.'

'Today you looked beautiful…' He was lying and she knew that. Nothing today she would have chosen for herself; the heavy satin dress, the ruffles, the embroidery were all way too elaborate for her full figure. Her curls had been dragged out then swept into a heavily lacquered French roll, her make-up heavy to appease the photographers, but, bathed now, still she felt as if she were wearing the mask as his fingers traced her cheeks.

Tears of bitterness and anger were filling her eyes as she recalled the last time he had done so and how readily she had succumbed and just *how* much she had adored him.

'Let's go to bed,' Effie said, her voice stilted and wooden, just wanting it over, wanting it done, hoping, praying she would produce heirs quickly and that his *duty* would soon be fulfilled. Then he wouldn't have to humiliate her by pretending once again that he actually might adore her.

She lay facing away from him, screwing her eyes closed at the indent of the mattress as he climbed into the bed beside her. The soapy scent of him wafted over her and she felt him stretch and relax muscles that must have ached after the day's exertions. It was hard to believe that in this lifetime she had once felt loved by him, that she had flown into his arms without thought or hesitation, sure his love would keep her safe.

What love?

Biting into her lip, she felt his hand brush her arms, and then down the curve of her waist, felt his lean hardness press into her as he lifted her hair and slowly, deeply kissed the back of her neck. His hand moved to the front of her nightdress and parted the laces and expertly began caressing her heavy breasts.

Only his tenderness had been an illusion, Effie reminded herself as she felt her nipples stiffen, simply a means to an end. She would not let his kisses move her.

'Effie...' He whispered her name in the shell of her ear. 'We can start again, this very night. There will be no divorce.'

'I accept that.' Her voice was wooden.

'Surely you can understand why I did what I had to do...'

'You could have told me—' she gave a shrill, mirthless laugh '—instead of fooling me into thinking you might love me...'

She turned and faced him, the eyes that had entranced him that night glistening with tears, the mouth that had teased him, had kissed him so intimately, twisted in anger and humiliation now. 'Did you laugh to yourself, Zakari, at how easy it was to beguile me?

Did it give you a glow of satisfaction as to how easily your fat maid succumbed to your charms?'

'You will not speak to me like that. I am your King.'

'I know that,' Effie spat. 'Over and over I know that now.' But always he could turn the tide. His mouth sought hers, his tongue probing, parting her lips, his knees nudging her milky thighs apart, his fingers trying to cajole her clitoris from its safe retreat.

And she hated her body that it responded, hated the silent beg of her nipples as his tongue neared, or the pit of want in her stomach as his fingers played on, moistening his path, yet she would not move, would not give in to him, though her body begged for her to surrender.

He was at her entrance now, still kissing her deeply, his erection sliding easily within, because though she hated herself for it her body was ripe for him, yet she lay there still as he moved inside her, knowing at some very deep level that if she forgave him now, then she would be lost for ever.

'Effie…' He was sliding over her, deep inside her. It took every ounce of resistance not to move with him. His tongue was caressing her ears and still she lay there, would not give him that piece of herself no matter how much she wanted to, no matter how he implored. 'Let us put it aside…' He was moving inside her, filling her, yet still she lay rigid.

'Let us go back to what we were, what we found.'

'We can't.'

His mouth moved higher, pausing when it tasted the salt of her tears.

'I want you as you were,' he demanded, only for Effie it was impossible.

'You want me to fake it?'

Enraged, he ceased unfinished.

'You are my wife,' Zakari roared. 'I accept you have been upset, but enough now. This has gone on long enough.' Zakari checked himself, conceded that perhaps it wasn't long enough and, though he couldn't quite believe he was doing it, he offered an extremely rare apology. 'I am truly sorry for all that I put you through, but as my wife you will have everything your heart desires. Why, then, can you not put things aside? Why can't you be the same woman you were when it was only for one night?'

'I trusted you then!' Effie's roar matched his. 'And I can never trust again!'

'So this is how it will be?' Zakari demanded.

'This is the only way it can be,' Effie sobbed.

'So, I am expected to masturbate into my wife—I am supposed to imagine that she is writhing beneath me as she once was.'

'Yes!' Effie answered, tears coursing down her cheeks, hating that it was so, but accepting that was all it could now be. 'If you want heirs—then yes!'

He was furious.

Always—always there was a solution, with women at least.

But not with Effie—or Stefania as she was now known.

She was the perfect wife—demure in public, and in private she did not tire him with senseless questions. In fact she made no demands on him at all.

But it was as if the fire had gone out of her.

No matter how expensive the gowns that she wore, she looked ill dressed.

The make-up did nothing to accentuate her features.

Everyone assumed he had married his fat, plain bride just to get the diamond.

Everyone including his fat, plain bride.

Everyone including himself—and yet…

Lying alone in his vast bed each night, knowing she was a door away, he would ball his fists at night beside him, tempted to summon her, but knowing it would be pointless.

He could arrange a mistress.

He didn't want one.

He wanted what they had once had.

Wanted everyone to see the beautiful Effie he had once witnessed, and Zakari wanted to meet her again too. He missed her chatter, missed her pretty eyes dancing as she spoke, those little jokes they had shared, and, God, he missed what he once had tasted, what they had once *been*.

There would be no heirs, till she changed her mind.

He would not take her dregs.

He would hold firm until she came to him, Zakari decided each night, before finally falling asleep.

Only to wake with a jolt before sunrise—realising it was hopeless.

Yes, Zakari was furious…

Only it was with himself.

CHAPTER ELEVEN

'WHAT will you do today?' Zakari asked, peering at her over his paper.

'I have to prepare for the opera tonight,' Effie answered, her cheeks burning at the thought of what lay ahead. A Greek prince was here with his fiancée and the Calistan royals were to be out in force tonight—a night at the opera, then dinner and dancing, away from the cameras on the royal yacht. For Effie it would be just another night of smouldering embarrassment, with cameras popping and everyone staring, knowing the ill-concealed smirks that would follow her along the red carpet as, yet again, the King's new wife got *everything* wrong. 'And there are my lessons, of course.'

He knew she found it humiliating being taught how to walk, how not to answer, how to greet dignitaries, but it was, of course, essential.

A rare smile flickered on his tired face as he imagined the Effie of old, laughing and chatting with a visiting royal, adding a little 'Don't be silly' when they paid her a compliment.

Not that she noticed his smile as, with her eyes down, she drank her coffee. She had been made up and dressed for breakfast, yet she felt awkward and cumbersome in yet another vast creation.

In an effort to play down her curves, the dressmaker just hid them in one shapeless piece of satin after the other. This one was exquisitely hand-embroidered, of course, but she didn't want rosebuds opening or butterflies fluttering on her bosoms, and Effie hated this latest design with a passion. She wished she had the nerve to ask Zakari if she might head to Aristo for a few days to visit some of the designer shops or even just send someone over, to give her some more modern, up-to-date advice.

Not that she should trouble him with something so trivial.

He had enough on his mind.

Since the explosion about the missing Stefani diamond had hit, Aristo had been in turmoil. That the Calistan King would now rule them had sent shock waves of fear, not just through the palace, but through the people, and the shock waves were being felt on Calista too.

The people of Calista were becoming increasingly convinced that the King's loyalties would now be divided, and there was considerable unrest that at every turn Zakari was trying to play down. But when yesterday some tribesmen elders from the desert had made a rare visit into town to voice their concerns, and had camped outside the palace to quietly register their protest, she had watched her husband falter. As Hassan had delivered the news Effie had seen the muscle pound in his cheek as he had glanced out of the palace window and witnessed his most beloved people, perhaps turning on him.

Zakari had dealt with it swiftly, of course. He had invited the elders into the palace and had met with them, had tried at length to appease them, but from his grim face when he had joined her for dinner last night Effie was sure that the meeting had not gone well.

He was grim-faced now, as he refused breakfast and just sipped on a second cup of coffee. Dressed in Western clothes, he had this restless energy about him this morning and, for Effie, his beauty had never been more savage.

In a black linen suit, he was a picture of suave elegance, his white shirt accentuating his olive skin. Though he was outwardly cool and unruffled, Effie could feel his tension, could hear the drum of his fingers on the table, the occasional hiss of irritation as he skim-read the papers. Today he was flying to Aristo, where he would meet with the current royal family who were also still reeling from the shock that, not only was the precious diamond now in the hands of Zakari, but Aegeus had had a long-term lover, who had produced a child.

Her.

'Today will be difficult…' she said, trying to offer some dutiful support.

It wasn't needed!

'Why?' Zakari shrugged. 'Christos's Legacy will be fulfilled—the diamond and the islands will be reunited. There will be one ruler now—a strong ruler! Surely that is better than Prince Alex who does not even want to be King?' His eyes challenged her to dare dispute.

'Still…' Effie gulped '…it *will* be hard for them.'

'I disagree,' he said through tight lips. 'Sebastian relinquished his right to the throne for love.' His lips sneered around the word as if he found it offensive.

'Alex would only be a reluctant King. His wife, Maria, has only recently had their baby.'

'Little Alexandra.' Effie smiled because she had read the news herself. 'After her father.'

Zakari didn't indulge in sentiment; he merely shrugged. 'Maria is passionate about her work—she would rather be designing crowns than wearing them. I am doing them all a favour.'

He tossed down his newspaper and stood. He would not kiss her goodbye; Effie knew that. Since she had refused to feign rapture at his lovemaking, there were no false displays of affection and no further attempts at lovemaking. Zakari was like a coiled spring, though, and she knew he wouldn't hold out for long, knew his sexual appetite was legendary. Each night she dreaded that it might be the night he gave in to the call of his body, that this might be the night when he finally took a mistress, but better that, Effie thought with sadness, than that she relent.

He had hurt her at her very core.

His lies, his deceit, the way he had toyed with her emotions for his gain, still chilled her to the marrow.

Yet still she loved him.

Yet still she was angry with him.

Hated that this beautiful, powerful, passionate man could at times be so void of emotion, could be so ruthless in his quest for power.

'Be gentle with her.'

She watched him stiffen at her words, and Effie held her breath as he turned around.

'With who?'

'With Queen Tia.' Effie took a deep breath. 'Please, be gentle with her.'

'This has surely been no great surprise to her,' Zakari said dismissively. 'Kings often take mistresses! Tia was deemed a suitable bride years before they even met. There was a long betrothal—it was about duty, not love. Tia knew from the start that it was a marriage of convenience…'

'No,' Effie whispered. 'No.' She said it again, only more strongly this time. 'Even if it started as duty for her, even if it was a marriage of convenience…' She swallowed hard. 'They had five children together, Zakari.'

'So might we—' Zakari shrugged '—when you stop this little game that you are playing.'

'It isn't a game,' Effie said. 'Men can detach, men can have sex, women can't.'

'You make no sense.'

'When a woman makes love…in that moment at least, she loves the man she is with.'

'You know this, do you?' Zakari sneered. 'From your five minutes of experience.'

'I know this.' Her eyes dared to hold his. 'It has nothing to do with experience—that is how women are. That is how I feel—trapped in a loveless marriage and supposed to turn it on like a tap. Tia *would* have loved him; so, please…' still she dared to hold his gaze as she refuted his words '…I am asking that you consider being gentle when you speak with her.'

He didn't respond and Effie sat as he stalked out, knowing he would not listen to her, knowing her words were probably already forgotten. She walked over to the window and watched the limousine that would deliver him to the runway and the royal jet that would carry him on the short flight to Aristo, and all Effie felt was relief.

Without Zakari's presence she could breathe, could

think more clearly, and Effie was determined to use every second that he was gone to get her head together.

'It is time for your lesson, Sheikha Stefania…' The words were delivered politely, but without respect or thought, in the same way her hair and clothes were attended to.

And Effie didn't want to play Sheikha today. She just wanted some time alone—to somehow come to terms with all that had changed in her life.

'Cancel the lessons,' Effie said as her maid's eyes widened. 'I have a headache.'

'But they are scheduled.'

'Unschedule them, then,' Effie snapped, cross and angry and scared, and just refusing to be a puppet today. Today, for a moment at least, she would pull the strings.

'I want my boxes brought to my room.'

'What boxes, Sheikha?'

'The boxes that were brought from my home—have them sent to my quarters. Then, I am not to be disturbed.' The maid was bowing as Effie swept out of the room, yet still trying to call her back.

'We need to prepare you for tonight…'

'Just have my things sent to my room.' At that moment Effie couldn't have cared less about a royal function that evening; she was having enough trouble getting through the next two minutes.

Her boxes containing her mother's things were duly delivered to her room. Effie could almost feel the anxiety in the maids and even Hassan was hovering nervously, everyone unsure how to react to the usually docile Effie, suddenly asserting her authority, especially when the King had just left!

Well, let them worry, Effie thought, eyeing the boxes

at her feet, ready now to face a task she had, for way too long, put off.

She wanted the truth—like it or not, she wanted to know the whole story!

Zakari was sitting in the back of yet another air-conditioned limousine, driving through the glitzy, modern streets of Aristo when he took the first call from a very worried Hassan, who informed him that Sheikha Stefania had not only cancelled her lessons, but was holed up in her room and demanding that they bring her mother's things to her.

Despite himself, Zakari gave a rare smile at the mini insurgence Effie had created.

He had known it would happen.

With every silent day that passed, with every night they spent apart, Zakari had known this day would come.

The bird he had trapped and caged was fluttering her wings, and, though it unsettled him, somehow he was proud.

Of her.

'You will obey her wishes,' Zakari said curtly to a perplexed Hassan.

His PA poured him a glass of icy water, and Zakari downed it in one gulp, but despite the refreshing chill, despite the cool air-conditioning in the luxury vehicle, Zakari was sweating as the Aristo palace loomed into view. Effie's words rang in his ears as the gates parted and the car swept along the impressive drive, and he saw Queen Tia standing on the steps to greet him, with some of her children at her side.

'Be gentle with her.'

As he walked up the palace steps the only thing

that worried Zakari was that without Effie it would never have entered his head.

He had loved her.

As Effie read the letters Aegeus had written to her mother, she felt as if her heart were being shaved layer by layer.

The agony, the impossibility, there on each fragile, time-wearied page. She read of the building pressure when Christos had died and the islands had been divided. When duty had called and Aegeus had been made King.

Read his private agony, revealed to her mother, as he had been forced to make the decision between his heart and his breeding and, reading on, with tears in her eyes she read his sad conclusion—for the sake of his people, breeding had won.

Yet—he *had* loved her.

Zakari had been right—Kionia was the royals' getaway, the one place they could escape to without fear of being seen or glimpsed and, despite Aegeus's marriage to Tia, they had made a pact and had met there on the eighteenth of May, each year.

Until she had been conceived, Effie realised, sad for both of them.

Sad for her mother who had chosen to raise her child alone rather than shame the King. Sad for her father who had never known of her existence.

Reaching into the box, pulling at a ribbon, Effie tried to locate her birth certificate, tried to tally up the dates…her face freezing as she realised it wasn't a birth certificate she was reading…

Sweat drenched her as the full impact of what she held in her hands, with aching slowness, hit home.

Aegeus had married her mother.

On May the eighteenth nineteen sixty-eight, her mother and father had married—sixteen years before she had been born. Effie searched on frantically; scrabbling through letters and certificates, she tried to make sense from the impossible.

This hadn't been some brief love affair; her parents had been married... On and on she searched, rummaging through the papers, sure that there must have been a discreet divorce, but when that search proved fruitless Effie read a fresh pile of letters, her heart stilling, her head pounding as she witnessed Aegeus's increasing anxiety in his desperate words, first begging her to respond, then imploring Lydia to stay quiet, that no one, *no one* must ever find out that there had been no divorce!

Effie stared wide-eyed and unblinking at the marriage certificate; for how long she sat there, she wasn't quite sure, but then, as if on autopilot, she picked up the phone.

Knew now what she would do.

It was like being pelted with tiny pebbles, while bracing for a rock. With every text, the message grew more urgent. Effie was now demanding designers and make-up artists to be flown in from Aristo. Yet, after a cursory glance, Zakari didn't respond to the messages, talking instead with Queen Tia as he had never thought he would.

'Excuse me, I am afraid that I have to take this call...' Zakari said, when he could ignore the summons for his attention no longer. He had three numbers he could be contacted on—a private one that was used regularly, which he had turned off for today, one for Hassan's and his top team's use, which, given the irritating messages, he had switched off too, leaving just a number that he could be reached on in exceptional emergencies only—and it was trilling frantically now.

Queen Tia had long ago dismissed the maids, and a long conversation had ensued between them, but now, when it would be negligent to ignore it, Zakari offered his apologies to Queen Tia, who politely excused herself as he answered the call.

'Your wife has requested the Stefani jewel be brought to her.'

Zakari didn't respond at first, his tongue on the roof of his mouth, a long silence ensuing as he surveyed the private living room where he had spent the afternoon.

Instead of the more formal portraits that lined the other walls of the palace, in here the walls were filled with simple family shots. Aegeus and Tia and their children. Alexander, Andreas, Katarina, Elissa and Sebastian, the man who had been groomed to be King, but whose love for his new wife, Cassie, had caused him to walk away from his birthright.

But was it his birthright?

What if Sebastian had turned down love, and decided instead to be King? Where would he stand now?

He might have lost it all.

Alex was being groomed for the role now, except he didn't want it…

Then there was Andreas, who had walked away from it all and now lived with the love of his life, Holly, in Australia…

He could feel the blood pounding in his temples as Hassan urged the King to react.

He had listened to Queen Tia today, just as he had listened to his wife.

Had seen the suffering in both women's eyes this very day and it had made him feel ill. All this pain, all this misery—and for what?

Power!

The power to hurt, to destroy, to ruin lives and families, to separate the islands only to now demand they unite, but in a bitter, false union.

'Of course, I have told her that it is impossible.' Hassan's voice was nauseating to Zakari's ears. 'I pretended that only you know the combination to the safe in the vault that contains the Stefani stone—'

'Stones,' Zakari corrected.

Two stones, two families, and all the agony that had been created.

'As I said earlier…' Zakari cleared his throat '…you will do whatever my wife wishes… Do not lie to her again.'

'But, Your Highness,' Hassan protested, which only served to inflame Zakari.

'You will give her the respect the wife of Sheikh King Zakari Al'Farisi deserves. The respect Sheikha Stefania deserves, which is something none of you have done these past weeks. What my wife demands she is to be given—I am not to be disturbed with such trivialities again.'

Striding out of the lounge room, scarcely able to believe the words he had just uttered, he met the kind, tired face of the Queen.

'Could we walk?' Zakari asked, feeling impossibly closed in, just desperate to escape, to drag fresh air into his lungs.

'That would be lovely,' Queen Tia answered calmly. 'I hope everything is okay?' she added later as they walked through the fragrant gardens.

'Apparently not!" He gave a tight smile.

'Then, I am sure you have it all under control.'

'Do we ever?' Zakari met her tired eyes.

'No,' Tia admitted.

'Yet we try,' Zakari insisted, only they both knew he was trying to convince himself.

'We do,' Tia agreed. 'Yet, when we accept we have no control, then life happens. Zakari, I know today has been difficult. I know it cannot have been easy for you to come and address such personal things with me…' Zakari actually felt a dull blush spread on his cheeks at how easy it *would* have been, had it not been for Effie. 'The news has not come as a shock to me. I always knew our marriage was one of convenience, that Aegeus's heart was distant. In those early years of our marriage I was quite sure that he had a mistress… For so long I felt trapped, my children were my existence. I hated that protocol, nannies, schooling took them away from me.' Zakari stared at her elegant face, her silver hair tied neatly back, the weary lines around her tired eyes, and his heart went out to this proud woman. 'May I share a secret, Zakari?'

'I would be honoured to hear it.'

'I loved my husband.' She gave a tight smile. 'Not at first. The first ten years of our marriage were difficult, and very miserable for me. I poured everything into my duties, and gave my heart to our children. Then one day…' they weren't walking now, just standing as this proud, dignified lady shared a piece of her heart '…it was as if my husband saw me for the first time, perhaps.

Not just as his wife, or his Queen, or his children's mother. I believe that in the end love grew between us. I believe that in the end my husband did love me.'

'He did.' Zakari stared into her soft brown eyes and he saw the sparkle of tears there. 'You will know that there was no love lost between Aegeus and I, but duty meant that we often found ourselves at functions together. I saw the pride on his face when he was with you, which cannot be manufactured. I heard him speak fondly of you…'

'Thank you,' Queen Tia whispered. 'I have been so nervous about today, so worried for my family; the last thing I expected was that this day would bring peace to my soul. I know there is a lot still to be discussed, details to be sorted, but thank you for being so gracious and kind.'

'There is someone else to thank for that.' Zakari gave a pensive smile and they started walking, a long, intensely private conversation ensuing as Zakari strolled with the matriarch of the Aristo family and talked in a way he had never thought he would, receiving guidance from a seemingly impossible source until it was sunset.

Later, as he contemplated the day's events, Zakari accepted that, though he might be guided by some unknown force, there was no control.

Guidance, yes—control, no.

He had caught her, caged her, and now the door was open.

He had broken her spirit, yet she had risen.

And, if she so chose, she was free to go.

The only revelation for Zakari was that he loved her.

It was fun really.

Ordering designers to fly over from Aristo, real designers who knew how to work with her curves, who lavished her with compliments and made her feel beautiful again.

And she'd had the top hair designer flown in too, a tiny man who fussed and cooed and gave her curls fit for a queen and who introduced Effie into the wondrous world of anti-frizz serum, her hair now a black glitter of snaky ringlets that framed her round face.

Then there was the make-up. Effie gaped in amazement that a shot of hot-pink blusher on her cheeks could transform her so, because, not only *didn't* it give her the cheekbones the Calistan make-up artist attempted daily to create, it actually made her proud of the two rosy apples that made her blue eyes glitter.

Oh, and then there was the heaven of eyeliner expertly applied!

Not that Hassan seemed impressed!

'The King is on his way back!' Hassan looked as if he might vomit as he attempted to be polite to Effie as he delivered the precious jewel. She was standing in a new dress, the design similar to the one she herself had created on her and Zakari's magical night in the desert, except this dress, she had been told, was an exclusive from the House of Kolovsky. Which meant little to Effie, except that it gave her a waist, and the stunning empress line displayed more daringly her creamy cleavage. The fabric was of the heaviest, softly brushed silk, and as for the colour—apparently the House of Kolovsky was renowned for their fabric, for the colours that changed, like opals, with a woman's mood! With every turn it changed, one moment dark purple, like the dress she had worn on the night Zakari had proposed, then next it shimmered as blue and clear as her own eyes, and then as she stepped back from the mirror again the dress changed, darkening to an inky black, as seductive, as mesmerising, as beguiling as Zakari's eyes as they looked into hers and lied.

'The King instructs that you are to be ready to leave—'

Effie cut him short with a smile that could only be seen in the mirror as she teased her hair into final shape.

'Oh, I'll be ready!'

And so she waited, lay on the bed and patiently waited till finally her moment came.

'We must leave if we are to be on time, but when we return, Effie…' He looked exhausted, his usually haughty face weary and tired, his eyes taking in the changes as the door was closed behind him. Effie, spectacularly beautiful, was lying on the bed draped in a soft silk dress, as beautiful now as she once had been, but with a dangerous glint in those wondrous blue eyes. 'We need to talk…'

'Then talk.'

'There is no time now! Duty—'

'Fine!' Like a lazy cat she slowly unfurled herself from the bed. His eyes followed her as she strolled across the room and headed for the dressing table. She saw his jaw tense as she picked up the Stefani diamond and unhurriedly clipped it around her neck, the stone falling into the familiar terrain of her cleavage.

Where it belonged.

'Oh, sorry.' Effie gave a sweet smile to his taut, pale face. 'I forgot we're in a hurry! Here…' She held out her mother's marriage certificate, watched the impatient shake of his head…

'There is no time for this now, Effie, if we are to get there…'

'Stefania,' she snapped. 'In fact, my correct title is Queen Stefania of Aristo…' Still she held out the marriage certificate and this time he took it, his face barely moving, his expression not changing as he took in the details. But since when did Zakari show emotion? Effie reminded herself.

'Your Highness…' Hassan's rapid knock was simultaneous with his entrance. 'If you are to make it on time—'

'We will not be attending!' The only indication that the news had floored him was a slight husk in his voice as he addressed his aide, but he quickly recovered, clearing his throat and stating his orders more clearly. 'Offer an excuse!' Zakari barked, then dismissed Hassan with a flick of the wrist.

But Effie had other ideas.

'Why would we not attend?' Effie smiled, picking up her tiny jewelled bag and heading out of the room. 'I'm looking forward to it!'

CHAPTER TWELVE

THERE is no presence more explosive than in a couple who have put a row on hold to go out.

Zakari, who had thought he knew women, realising this day and night that there were many lessons still to be learnt. The tender, yet heartfelt apology he had hoped to deliver after talking with Tia was, he realised, too little, too late, and just woefully inadequate now.

Like a firecracker with the tape lit, Effie sat fizzing beside him, tapping her foot to an unheard beat, her eyes glittering. Instead of her usual nerves and trepidation as they approached the gathered crowd that would welcome them, as the car slid to a halt Zakari watched as a small, satisfied smile parted her rouged lips.

He heard the gasp of the crowd as Effie stepped onto the red carpet, the explosion of cameras as they captured the woman, as they witnessed for the first time the beauty he had always seen.

Oh, a firecracker was the wrong description, Zakari soon realised.

Firecrackers exploded in an instant, whereas Effie fizzed and smouldered the whole night long.

She was like a Catherine wheel, Zakari decided—

beautiful, mesmerising, entrancing, yet dangerous to touch. Like moths to a flame, she held everyone's attention, her curls bobbing, her throat creamy white as she threw her head back and laughed at a joke, the jewel between her breasts a mere shadow to the woman who wore it tonight.

In a matter of hours she had become a woman—all woman.

For Zakari the opera was excruciating. Sitting beside a delighted Effie, who appeared entranced—dum-diddy-umming to 'Carmen Prelude,' laughing, crying throughout the lavish presentation, even talking to him in the interval, yet the dangerous game she was playing was right there in her eyes, and as the night progressed Zakari actually worked out her strange rules.

She was showing him.

Showing him all she could have been.

Showing him what now he could never, ever have.

'It has been a wonderful night!' Kalila smiled warmly to Effie as the royals prepared to make their exit to the cars.

'Really?' Aarif rolled his eyes. 'I am looking forward to eating. What about you, Zakari?'

'We won't be coming to the yacht.'

'But you're expected!' Aarif said.

'My wife is not feeling well!' Zakari snapped, taking a smiling Effie's hand. Tonight he was grateful for his status as it allowed him to exit first, because Effie was like the firecracker again now—ready to explode. 'She has a headache.'

There was a recklessness to her; he could feel it coursing through her fingers as he held them, could taste it in the very air that he breathed, heard it as for the first time she challenged him publicly.

'Do I?' The giggle that followed had a slightly manic ring to it. 'Well, if you say I have a headache then I guess I must!'

The car ride home was appalling.

The silence thick with tension, both spilling out of the car and practically running inside, Zakari throwing his jacket to a waiting maid, then taking the steps two, three at a time, then turning to face her as she entered his room.

Angry with her, furious with her, yet wanting her.

'Our troubles are not to enter the public arena. You are never to speak like that to me in public again!'

'I won't!' Effie responded, her lips curling with suppressed anger. 'Because we will never be seen in public together again, Zakari.'

He had known this was coming, not just because of the marriage certificate Effie had produced tonight, but from the moment he had told her his truth on the balcony, he had known this moment would come—and he was loath to face it, but for different reasons now. 'Effie, I know there are things to discuss.'

'So you're suddenly interested in what I have to say, now that I'm not Aegeus's bastard child, now my opinion counts!'

'I told you as soon as I came home that we needed to talk. I have been thinking about you, about us, all day.'

'Really?' Wide-eyed with disbelief, she challenged him, stood tall so he might see what he never, ever would have. *That* was supposed to be her pleasure, only the rush of satisfaction she had been expecting never came. 'Well, I've been thinking too—I am leaving you,

Zakari. I am taking the stone that is rightfully mine and leaving tonight for Aristo. I am quite sure you will try and fight me,' Effie added before he could. 'After all, I signed the stone over to you, but at the time of signing I didn't know its worth… Now, as Queen, I will get the best legal advice on Aristo.'

'You will destroy two islands with our fighting,' Zakari pointed out.

'It didn't stop you…' For a second she faltered, his words hitting their mark, but she dismissed them with a shake of her head. 'You don't care about the people of Aristo. It is all about power to you.'

'It was!' Zakari caught her wrist as she made to leave. 'As I said, Effie, all day I have thought of you. All day with Queen Tia I have been thinking of you and wanting to say that I am truly sorry for what I did to you—for my deceit. I now finally understand just how much I hurt you…'

'Oh, you understand now, do you?'

'Effie.' He took her tense hands in his and held them, stared into her eyes as he said the words he had been longing to say the whole wretched night. 'I realise that I love you…'

'Bastard!' She spat, spat at his face again, and yet still he didn't flinch. 'Now you decide that you love me. Now, when I take away your power, you suddenly decide that you love me after all. Do you think I am so stupid, Zakari?' She thumped his chest, but still he didn't flinch. 'Do you think I might fall for your empty words again, that you could humiliate me all over again and I would just take it?'

'From the day Anya told me her truth, I have hated Aegeus.' Zakari stood tall and proud as she raged around him, as she paced the floor, deflecting his words, refusing to let him in. 'I have hated Aegeus with a depth that was as ferocious as it was dangerous. I realise now the damage that hatred has caused, but at the time I thought I had reason.'

'Because Aegeus ruled Aristo, because you craved power—'

'No.' Zakari shook his head, real honesty just a breath away, and he knew it was time to reveal, knew he could no longer hold the black secret inside—knew that time was over. 'Aegeus and Anya were half brother and sister. Christos doted on Anya, yet male primogeniture meant that Aegeus would be King.'

'I know all that.' Effie shook her head.

'There was always jealousy, always there was rivalry between them, but when Christos decided the islands would be split…it became worse.'

'I know all that,' Effie repeated through clenched teeth, sitting on the bed, scrunching her hair in her hands, unsure of his tactics, unsure what lies would be delivered to convince her to stay.

'Anya fell pregnant to a groundkeeper…'

Effie felt her heart still. She knew how highly Zakari thought of his stepmother, was sure, *almost* sure that he would never shame her memory with such a lie, but this was Zakari she was dealing with, Effie reminded herself, a ruthless, maverick man who would say anything, do anything to reach his goals, and she wouldn't forget that for a moment.

'Aegeus was furious, furious at the shame she would bring to the family, there was a fight—Aegeus struck her, she stumbled backwards and fell, and lost the baby…' Effie could feel the make-up sliding down her cheeks as it mingled with her tears, reminding herself that even if he was telling the truth, it didn't right his wrongs. 'Anya was the most wonderful stepmother, yet she would have given anything to be a mother to her own child. She told me that, told me how my father and his children filled her soul with happiness, how proud she was that we were her heirs, yet she also told me of her pain—that because of what Aegeus did, she could not bear children of her own. I saw her pain and her sadness and I swore revenge. Since that day it is all I have craved and in my quest for that I have destroyed people. I have destroyed and broken you—you, the woman I love, and now Tia. When she finds out the truth…' Zakari closed his eyes in dread at what the news would do to that proud, dignified woman he had spent the day with today. 'I am no better than Aegeus…'

'You almost had me convinced!' Effie stood up, wiped the tears from her face with shaking hands, her mouth twisted in pain and bitterness. 'You almost had me convinced, but not quite. You don't learn, do you?' She jabbed a finger at his chest. 'Had you told me it was the diamond you wanted, had you told me it was a marriage of convenience, I could have accepted it. Even now, when you tell me about Anya and Aegeus, I can understand what drives you, why you have found it so impossible to forgive him, but to again say you love me…' The sob that escaped from her lips came from somewhere so deep, and was so raw, so loaded with pain, that only now did Zakari flinch, his hand moving to comfort her, but she flicked it off.

'I loved you so much.' Effie sobbed her humiliation, almost vomited it out at his feet. 'So much that I could even have accepted that you didn't love me. When we made love that first night, I accepted the terms, I was happy with that, but then you lied, then—you—let—me—think—that—you—loved—me—too…' She spat each word out, because she burnt, just burnt with shame and humiliation as she remembered taking him in her mouth and writhing in his hands. She remembered accepting his endearments, ashamed, just bitterly, bitterly ashamed that she had actually thought for that slice of time that she was, to him, beautiful. 'And now you lie again… Now, when you have so much to lose, suddenly you decide that you love me…'

'I do,' Zakari insisted. 'Effie, today I realised, as much as I loathed him, Aegeus and I are the same, we are no different.'

'You mean you both have a penchant for palace maids!' Effie scoffed.

'No.' Zakari shook his head, implored her with his eyes to just believe. 'He loved the mother, I love the daughter.'

'And you both hurt the women you say that you loved,' Effie sobbed. 'Some wounds cannot heal, Zakari.'

'They might—with time.'

'No.' She shook her head, tears pooling in her eyes as Zakari surveyed the damage he had done, the pain he had inflicted, as the woman he loved turned to leave. 'I will have my things sent for.'

'You're leaving now?' Panic gripped him. If he could just tell her again, just have one night to convince her, then maybe, maybe… He grabbed at her arm, tried to halt her progress. 'It is too late.'

'Much, much too late,' Effie retorted, shaking him off, her beautiful features now twisted in bitterness. 'A servant who has two masters is lying to one of them!' She watched his face pale as she jeered him with the old

Arabic proverb. 'It's all just a power trip to you! How did you think you could serve the people of Aristo, when your heart belongs to Calista? When all you want from them is your revenge!'

'Silence!' Zakari roared, and willingly she agreed.

'Silence is all you will get from now on from Aristo and its Queen!' Effie shouted. Fleeing from his room, fleeing from the man she loved, because if she stayed a second more Effie knew she'd give in, knew that she might accept his lies, rather than live a life without him.

'Sheikha Stefania…' Hassan scuttled towards her as she raced down the stairs '…I trust everything is okay.'

'Everything is *not* okay,' Effie started, her mouth opening to demand the royal plane, to alert the Aristo palace of her arrival, then closing again.

Braver with Zakari than without him.

'I need to think…'

'Of course.' Hassan bowed, his voice supremely calm, but it only exacerbated her more. Oh, she knew she looked a sight, her face no doubt streaked with tears and make-up, her body shivering as her world collapsed, but if she could just have five minutes alone she would regain control, could work out what to do!

'Alone!' she insisted, being led like a deranged patient to a study as a maid opened the door, eyes duly lowered as Hassan guided her in. 'You will not discuss my whereabouts with the King.'

Alone, she tried to gather her thoughts, but it was impossible to do that here.

Here in the very room they had been married—where he had made her sign over the diamond.

Here, where she had trusted him.

The French windows in the study opened to the now

dark palace gardens; she could hear the fountains gently rolling, smell the fragrant air, and she stepped out, dragging the cool night air in, but it didn't soothe. Still she felt stifled, closed in…

The huge stone fences, the vast metal gates at the garden's edge, even the vast garden only closeted her further, yet behind them, beyond them was the desert…

That was where Zakari went, Effie thought, to clear his head, when he needed guidance, and she actually understood his reasoning now, could see the desert's appeal.

And it was a palace, not a prison, Effie realised as she turned a heavy handle and the gate opened. It was designed to keep people out, not in. Effie breathed as she took her first tentative step towards freedom. Hearing the gate close behind her, Effie tried the handle once, knowing exactly what she would find, knowing it would be locked, and relieved that it was.

And then she ran.

The cobbled path at the palace's rear perimeter gave way in a matter of moments to the soft sands of the desert, only she was too angry to be frightened.

Angry with Zakari and his lies, Effie thought, taking off one shoe and hurling it into the night. She screamed in anguish, hurling abuse as if she were deranged.

But she was just angry!

Angry with her mother too, Effie let out a long-suppressed keening wail as she hurled off her other shoe. She was so angry with her mother for leaving her without ever revealing the truth, for denying her all those years to the right to her personal history, for making her hear it unarmed and unaware.

Just angry, so very angry at the world as she ran.

With her father for cheating, for lying, for his bigamy and the damage it would now wreak.

And she was angry with herself…

The desert didn't scare her… She just ran into it, ran through it, slicing it with her rage. It could claim her if it wished; they could find her in fifty years for all she cared, and grab their precious jewel from her skeleton's neck, but for now she ran, just ran as far away as she could, because Effie knew if she didn't run, then she might go back.

Might still go back.

Spent, she sank to the sandy floor and wept.

Anger fading to bemusement that she could ever think of going back to him after the way he had treated her.

That after all the shame, all the pain that had been inflicted, still she wanted to return.

Surely closing her eyes and make-believing that he loved her was better than being without him.

How, she begged to the darkness, could she be better off without him, when she loved him to her very core?

How was it better to sleep alone than with the man she loved?

She could see the lights of the palace blinking in the distance and she wanted to go back, wanted every tiny part of Zakari he was prepared to give. She wanted his feigned kisses, his body pressed to hers and she wanted to believe that smile he occasionally gave was truly for her, and she was bitterly ashamed of her want.

Turning her back, she hugged her knees and willed dignity to return.

She begged for the craving to pass. She knew from experience that it would—just as it had when the handle had turned on her locked bedroom door that night, just as it had so many nights when her body had thrummed for her to join him, just as it had when he had kissed her at the polo match, Effie reminded herself, rocking through the craving—just as it had when he'd been inside her on their wedding night…

It would pass, Effie told herself, for the millionth time.

Soon it would pass.

CHAPTER THIRTEEN

THE same but different.

In a different land, in a different time, Zakari could remember walking into his father's bedroom, seeing him staring out to distant, unseen sands, on the night his mother, Princess Saffiya Al'Farisi, had died. Zafir's lusty, newborn cries being hushed by a wet nurse.

Zafir the only one permitted to weep.

'Stay strong!' His father, Sheikh Ashraf, had squeezed his son's shoulder, when Zakari had wanted to be held. 'It is not for us to demand answers.'

And later, in this very room where he stood now, his father had demanded the same of him as his new wife, Anya, lay weeping on the bed, little Zafir lost and missing.

The same but different.

A flash of something moving in the garden caught his eyes, but Zakari wasn't concentrating; the guards would sort it out. Later he could hear shouting, perhaps a scuffle would ensue, but he just didn't care, listened as the mad, demented ranting faded into the distance and stared at the land that had brought him so much comfort, and wished it could bring some now.

Yes, it was the same but different.

Because this king wept.

'Your Highness…' Hassan bowed as he entered.

'I said I was not to be disturbed!' Zakari snapped, refusing to turn, still too proud to let a servant see him cry.

'I understand that.' He was practically prostrate, bowing in deep apology, yet frantic all the same. 'Sheikha Stefania ordered that I not discuss her whereabouts, but, Your Highness, she has gone—'

'I know that!' He should feel shame, should feel anger, but all he felt was sad, hollow and horribly, horribly empty.

'We cannot just let her!' Hassan implored.

'It is her choice.' Zakari shook his head wearily. 'It is her right to go.'

'But anything could happen!' Hassan pleaded.

'It probably will.' Zakari shrugged, not caring in this moment about the chaos that surely lay ahead, for now just consumed with missing Effie.

'But we cannot just leave her alone in the desert!' Hassan whimpered as the blood in Zakari's veins froze.

'She's in the desert?' Zakari's voice was like a whip cracking.

'She has run out of the palace gardens and into the desert.' Hassan's words hit him in the back as he ran through the palace, propelling him on. 'There was a disturbance and the guards checked the gates, but found nothing, but she is not in the study or her room—'

'She has not gone to Aristo?'

'No! She was distressed. I left her alone in the study and she hasn't been seen since. She's been gone for over an hour. We cannot find her!'

* * *

Zakari had never feared the desert. He had respected it, but never feared it—yet it terrified him now.

Standing on its edges, staring out into the black sky, the sliver of a new moon did nothing to light it—just a black, endless emptiness. The air was cold that would only grow colder, and the thought of Effie out there had Sheikh King Zakari Al'Farisi, for the first time in his life, tasting fear, an alien panic rising in him at the prospect of the land he loved claiming the woman he loved more.

His helicopter lifted into the sky.

A skilled pilot, Zakari took control as Hassan worked the searchlight, the beam splitting the darkness as they scoured the savage land for her.

Not for the diamond, not for Queen Stefania of Aristo, but for Effie.

His Effie, who had loved him.

Had utterly and completely loved him as he, Zakari fast realised, had always utterly and completely loved her.

She would be terrified.

He shivered at the thought of the dogs the palace guards would be running out into the desert now, barking and snarling as they tracked her scent, and he prayed he would get there first, before the other helicopters that would be lifting into the sky soon. All he could think of was her, little and out there alone.

'There,' Hassan shrieked for maybe the twentieth time. 'Back there.' Zakari hovered in the sky as Hassan moved the beam, trying to locate the shadow he had thought he had seen, but there had been so many false sightings that Zakari didn't dare hope—till he saw her. This pale dot beneath him, coming more into focus as the chopper lowered: Effie sitting on the sandy floor, face down and hugging her knees.

Yes, that was why he hated falconry, Zakari thought again as he circled his prey. He didn't feel powerful, he didn't want to pounce, he just wanted her to be safe, wanted one more chance to tell her that he loved her and let her know that she was free.

'Call everyone off!' Zakari delivered his orders through his mouthpiece. 'Hassan, turn off the beam.'

It did pass…

Effie could hear the bark of dogs in the faraway distance, could hear the chopper, and see its beam of light as it scoured the desert for its jewel.

He could have it.

Taking off the necklace, she held it in her palm ready to hand to him.

She could feel the blizzard of sand whipping her cheeks as it landed, and she held the jewel to her heart one final time as Zakari approached, not once looking up as she willed the desert to tell her what she should do.

'Does she have to know?' Effie didn't look over as he sat down beside her. 'If I give you the stone, if I stay as your wife, if we carry on as before…'

'We can't carry on as before,' Zakari said. 'If there is one thing I have learnt these past weeks, it is that the truth always catches up.'

'I can't do it to Queen Tia,' Effie whispered. 'I meant it when I said I was going, but when I think of her…'

'You are a gentle, kind person,' Zakari said. 'That is why this is all so hard for you.'

'And I couldn't stay in the palace with you,' Effie

said, shaking her head at the hopelessness of it all, 'but if that is my duty…'

'Forget duty,' Zakari said, for the first time in his life. Shocked at his statement, Effie turned and looked at him. 'Forget duty and protocol, for a moment at least… Here in the desert, truth can be revealed.'

'Take it.' Effie held out her hand and opened it. 'Please, just take it.'

Which he did.

He took the stone he had so desperately searched for, took the power and the revenge he had craved, and without hesitation held it up to her neck, fiddled with the clasp for a moment, till the stone hung heavy and beautiful where it belonged.

'I could rule alone, but I know I will rule more wisely with you—with the kind, sweet and sexy woman that you are beside me.' He gave her a rare smile, and it wasn't mocking; it was nothing but gentle. 'Kings do not make their maids coffee,' Zakari said, 'no matter how bitterly they cry. Do you remember that, Effie?'

'Of course I do.'

'Kings do not speak of their fears and grief with servants or with anyone… I realise that I loved you then as I love you now.'

Still she shook her head.

'Kings do not make love to maids. They have sex…' with one shrug of those wide shoulders he dismissed every previous encounter, discounted them all as re-alisation hit '…but they do not make love.' For the first time he held her, placed his arm around her shoulder and pulled her cold body into him. 'Even if I didn't know it at the time, we made love that night, Effie.'

How she wanted to believe him.

And how scared she was to believe him.

'When I brought you back to the palace, my aides said that I did not have to marry you, that we could retrieve the stone, that you would have no choice but to hand it back. They said that it hadn't been Aegeus's to give to your mother—everyone was delighted, everyone except me. So I told them I had slept with you.'

'You told them.' Effie winced into his chest.

'That was not a problem apparently…' he held her tight, spoke into her hair, stroked and soothed her shivering, trembling body '…until I revealed that I had not used protection. That you might be carrying my child.'

'I wasn't, though.'

'I did not want to wait to find out,' Zakari said, 'because then you might go.' His proud, liquid-smooth voice faltered for a moment. 'I did not want to lose you. I thought this way I could keep you. Except you do not want to be kept, do you?'

He closed his eyes in bliss as her head shook on his chest. Here was the one woman in the world who loved him for him, not for his title, but in spite of it.

'You really would live in a tent, wouldn't you?'

'I'd prefer your luxury tent, though…' for the first time since their wedding night she let out a giggle, and it was the most beautiful sound he had ever heard '…rather than the one I had in mind, but, yes, Zakari—if I believed you loved me, I'd move to the end of the earth to be with you.'

'Why don't I take you now to my tent?' Zakari lifted her chin till she looked at him. 'Why don't we go there now, and we will stay for however long it takes for me to convince you that I love you?'

'We can't.' Effie gave a shocked gasp. Oh, it sounded

wonderful, but it was impossible all the same. 'We have to sort things out—what we are going to do, how we will tell Queen Tia…' Her heart quickened with the horror of all that lay ahead, and then he kissed her, this slow, measured kiss that was so tender, and so utterly loaded with love, they didn't need to hide away till he convinced her, because he already had.

'I have the marriage certificate with me,' Zakari said. 'No one is going to find out just yet… We will work it out together. For the first time in my life, duty can wait. Have you any idea how good it feels to say that?'

'Have you any idea how good it feels to hear it?' Effie said. 'So,' she teased him with a smile, 'if we do go to your tent, tell me again, how are you going to convince me that you love me?'

'A bit like this…' He kissed her again, laid her down on the sand, and kissed her harder this time, then he pulled back.

'That's not very convincing,' Effie grumbled, because if he did love her, if he really, *really* loved her, then surely he should be making glorious love to her right here and now. She was playing with the buttons on his shirt, so she could get right to that sexy chest, to feel the skin that she had craved for so long… 'Make love to me, Zakari…'

'Of course.' He smiled down at her, his lips parting as he gave her the smile that would for ever melt her heart. 'But should I tell Hassan to return in a little while, or just hope he averts his eyes?'

'Ow!'

He loved that she blushed, loved that she forgot about staff and protocol, that she could push it all aside at times, to get to what really mattered.

'Come on, you.' He stood up and brushed himself down, then offered her his hands and pulled her up beside him. Then he held her hand as they walked towards the helicopter. 'Our tent awaits.'

EPILOGUE

EFFIE stared out of the vast windows, to the infinity pool that stretched into the rough waters that linked the two islands and beyond to Calista.

Shaking with nerves, somehow she was poised as her king entered, the maids who had bathed, oiled and dressed her dispersing as Zakari walked in dressed in full military uniform. He cut an imposing figure, but unlike her wedding day, her nerves were not for him, but for the huge commitment she would undertake today.

'You look beautiful.'

She did…standing in the very room in which she undoubtedly had been conceived, Effie tried to comprehend all that had happened over these past few months. In the seven months since their marriage the hate Zakari had borne for Aegeus had been diminished by his love for his bride.

Alex's coronation had been scheduled for January, but with all that had taken place, and the adjustments that had needed to be made, Effie's coronation had been set for May.

The eighteenth of May, as it turned out.

The anniversary of her parents' marriage.

She was wearing a floor-length golden gown, finely woven strands of golden silk making a stunning emphasis of her curves. Each curl of her hair had been painstakingly attended to by her favourite hairdresser, her hair loosely but, oh, so carefully piled on top of her head, while the occasional ringlet that had been threaded with a single strand of gold silk tumbled down.

'Beauty will not make me a wise ruler.' She stared down at the letter she was holding. 'It is from Sebastian and Cassie.' Effie swallowed hard, butterflies dancing in her chest as she contemplated all she was taking on. 'He was groomed to be King. This should have been his day. How can I possibly do it better than him?'

'It is your birthright, whether you like it or not,' Zakari said gently. 'I have struggled with the same question, but from a different angle. I was not born to be King and yet, I am. Sometimes life takes a turn and all we can do is follow the new path.'

'Oh!' Effie blinked in surprise. 'That is what Sebastian said. You two are quite similar in your views.'

'I always thought so too. I always admired Sebastian,' Zakari said. 'Though I felt I should be ruler, still I admired him, still I knew he would rule well. And while I thought we shared the same views, I did not understand why he would renounce the throne for love. I never thought I would understand it.' He stared over at Effie, love blazing in his haughty proud face as he gazed at his lover, his wife and his Queen and knew then that the former two were the ones that mattered most. 'I do now.'

As Effie handed him the letter he read it carefully

without comment, before folding it up and handing it back to her.

'He sounds very happy.'

'He is.' Effie smiled. 'When he and Cassie declined the invitation I thought there may be some bitterness—I was wrong. They had a very good reason for staying away—their second child is due today!'

'That cannot be a coincidence.' Zakari smiled. 'Today is about moving forward, accepting new responsibility, new challenges…'

'With grace!' Effie whispered.

'Always with grace…' He traced the apple of her cheek. 'You can do this—you are wise and you are kind and you were born for this,' Zakari said firmly, because she was.

Queen Tia's shame at her bigamous marriage, that her children were illegitimate, somehow, under Effie's gentle guidance, had been tempered. Resentment and fears quashed as Effie herself, with Zakari by her side, had carefully and sensitively revealed the news.

Effie, who had held Tia as her life had fallen apart.

Zakari, who had stepped in then and helped Tia build it up again.

'Your secret is your captive,' Zakari had told her, as together they had faced a public who had wanted answers. 'So set it free!'

Because there could be no whispers and innuendo when dark secrets were brought out and offered to the scrutiny of light.

Tia's shame had faded when the man who would, without his Queen, have crushed them in the palm of his hands, instead stood proud beside the Karedes family. In a benevolent but utterly, intrinsically right gesture, Zakari and Effie had insisted that the Karedes family retain their royal status, had reassured them that all that they were—the family they had built, the people they had served—still remained.

That the people of Aristo loved and needed them too.

'Do you know how differently things would have been without you?' He stared into her blue, blue eyes. 'You were born for this. Wisdom flows in your veins, and the Kingdom of Adamas is better for having you.'

'You will guide me, though?'

'We will guide each other.'

'Tell me again what will happen…' Nerves were starting to catch up with her now.

'We will ride through the streets of Aristo and you will wave and acknowledge the people—your people. Then, we will arrive at the palace and the coronation will take place as rehearsed. After there will be formal speeches, then dinner and a party where you will more personally greet all the dignitaries…' He smiled at her pale features. 'It will be an exhausting day.'

'Your speech is prepared?' Effie checked, seeing the bob of his Adam's apple and for the first time realising that he was nervous too.

'I am ready.' He kissed her cool cheek, held her trembling in his strong arms as they faced the two islands' biggest day.

The power he had sought, the revenge he had demanded, forgotten now.

'Together we will rule the Kingdom of Adamas and one day the jewels will be reunited, as will the islands. Maria has already started to make designs for the new coronation crown, that, God willing, our heir will one day wear.' He watched a flicker of something pass over her features…

'Effie?'

'Stefania,' she corrected with a wry smile. 'You must get used to calling me that now.'

'Are you okay?'

'Of course.'

'It will happen in time.'

'I know.' She smiled.

'And if it doesn't, that will not change us.'

'I know that too.'

'You would tell me if there was something worrying you? I will do everything I can to make today as easy on you as possible…'

'I know that.'

How she wanted to tell him.

They had been married for seven months now and though it was still early days, with each month that had passed Effie had held her breath, then let it out in disappointment. Everyone seemed to be pregnant or having babies, and though Zakari had made no comment, though she felt safe in his love, she wanted their baby so badly. Wanted the heir the kingdom needed and now it was happening.

The royal doctor had examined her yesterday evening and had confirmed the precious truth—yet there hadn't been a moment to tell Zakari. A pre-coronation function had seen them fall into bed at 2:00 a.m., only to be up at 5:00 to prepare for this day, and the news she wanted to impart was surely too precious to be hurried. There was so much going on today, so many details and so many things to attend to. Tonight, Effie decided, she would tell him tonight, when they were truly alone, when duty, at least for a moment, had been done and it was solely about them, she would tell him.

'Your Highnesses…'

The bedroom door was opened—privacy had no place in this day—and, still holding on to her precious secret, Effie took her husband's arm, grateful she could lean on him, knowing he was there beside her.

The staff lined the hallway, and as the palace doors opened Effie caught her breath.

She had been through the plans over and over, but nothing could ever have prepared her for the sight of the cars, the motorbikes and the cheers from the palace gates.

They were driven in a cream open-topped car, preceded by motorbikes, and security cars brought up the behind. Well-wishers lined every inch of the streets on the long drive to the palace, their cheers and waves growing louder and more frantic as the crowd deepened the closer they got.

Frequently they stood. And she smiled at them all, waved back at every face she could see as Zakari did the same.

The people were running, cheering, craning their heads for a long glimpse of the beautiful royal couple.

'They are cheering for you,' Zakari said. 'Your people are happy.'

'They know we will do well. They know that the Kingdom of Adamas is safe.'

Finally they were at the palace.

Effie was shaking with nerves, but Zakari held her hand as they were greeted with an honour guard, but then it was time for him to let go.

This walk she must make alone.

'Look at you!' Eleni held her for a moment as Zakari took his place, as the last of the vital details were put into place. 'You look stunning.'

'I'm scared,' Effie admitted, letting Eleni hold her, so glad for the friendship and wisdom her sister-in-law so readily gave.

'I am terrified too…' Kalila came over. Always, to Effie, she had seemed to stand slightly apart, but suddenly they were close as Effie saw that this beauty, this wonder woman who had been bred to be Zakari's Queen, now stood, nine months pregnant and terrified. 'What if my waters break during the service?'

Effie gave a shocked giggle and realised at that moment they were all the same, a group of women, of friends who were all in their own way doing their best.

'I'll have a seizure!' Eleni proudly announced. 'If your waters pop, I promise I will collapse to the floor and create such a scene, no one will even notice the puddle!'

'Promise?' Kalila checked, a smile edging on her lips.

'We're in this together,' Eleni said, holding Effie's hand as the band grew louder.

'They are waiting.' Hassan spoke kindly to her now as Kalila and Eleni faded away and took their places beside their husbands.

Hassan was a resource she had never thought she would tap, yet, in desperate times, Effie tapped it now.

'I'm scared, Hassan.'

'Why?' Hassan asked.

'Because I'm not good enough!' Through shivering teeth she admitted the truth.

'You are better than good.' Hassan stared at the Queen of Aristo, then voiced his own truth. 'I am proud to serve you.'

'How?' Effie begged as the presentation music started, as at the final hurdle she faltered. 'How, when I have no education, when I am nothing more than a palace maid, can you be proud to serve me, can you trust in me to be right?'

'Because you are,' Hassan answered simply, then repeated it. 'Because you are.'

Every head turned.

Except Effie's.

Oh, she wanted to seek out Zakari, yet she must stare fixedly ahead as she took the longest walk of her life.

Her husband waiting by the Calistan throne ahead as she walked for this moment alone.

Towards Queen Tia.

In Effie's eyes, she was the most beautiful and elegant of them all.

She was the one who would place the crown on her head.

And fear, terror, nerves were momentarily forgotten as she met those kind brown eyes.

She closed her eyes as the judge read out the words, as a baby's cry soared to the roof of the palace and she felt the weight of the crown as Queen Tia placed it on her head, the jewel her mother had loved safely back in the Aristan crown now, and Effie suddenly knew then— knew that she could do this.

Knew she would falter at times, knew that wrong decisions would be made, but she also knew she would do her best.

And her best—as Effie stood with the help of Queen Tia's hand, and adjusted to the new weight she carried—was all her people asked of her.

Her best was the best she could give.

* * *

The formal dinner took for ever. The speeches even longer, and as for the first time Effie stood to address her people, she stammered out her speech, could feel the beads of sweat rising on her forehead as she made heavy work of the words that blurred in front of her.

She was going to be sick.

Effie knew that if she stood for a single moment longer…well, it didn't bear thinking about, so quickly, through pale lips, she addressed the expectant room.

'I ask that you hear my husband…'

'You have not finished your speech!' Zakari frowned.

'Speak for me, Zakari,' she urged.

'They need you,' Zakari started, but his frown changed to one of concern when he saw her pale face, and as she sat down Zakari stood. The short speech he had written would not suffice here, and, taking a deep breath, he spoke from the heart.

'Your Majesties, dignitaries, Comrades in Arms…' Zakari made light work of the necessary introductions, and then it was time for truth. 'I speak not for my wife, but with my wife…

'My stepmother, Queen Anya Al'Farisi of Calista, was amongst the wisest of women and yet even she made mistakes.'

Zakari stared at the gathering and gave a dry smile.

'When I was fourteen she inadvertently purchased for me the teachers' version of my school textbooks. For one year I had all the answers. I had the best education, I went to the finest school, yet for one year I did not need to listen, because I had all the answers. There was no homework that year, and there were no detentions because I was never wrong—I just turned to the back of the book.'

The gathering laughed at his admission.

'But the next year, when I didn't have the answers to hand, and was lacking a year of education, I was beaten for failing.'

He returned the smile of the gathering.

'I had learnt nothing that year. I had all the answers—yet I learnt nothing.'

The room wasn't smiling now, every face serious as Zakari moved straight to the necessary point. For if they were all to move on, there were some final things that needed to be said.

'I knew King Christos's Legacy by heart, yet only now do I truly understand it. Like the teenager I once was, I thought I had all the answers, yet I see now I lacked wisdom...' His gaze fell on his wife. ' Now, I have been blessed with wisdom...

'All of us are blessed...' Zakari said, pausing for a moment as the crowd thundered their applause, then stilled to let him continue.

'All of us have learnt that truth, love and kindness always win. This is how we will build the Kingdom of Adamas. This is how we will prosper and stay for ever strong.'

He raised his glass as the people did the same and everyone followed. 'I toast the Queen of Aristo—long may she rule.'

The line was daunting.

Kings and queens, princes and princesses from Europe, the Middle East, from lands Effie hadn't even heard of, all lined up to greet her.

The first few, though, were not so daunting.

The Aristo royals, at Effie's request, were the ones that greeted her first.

Queen Tia, holding her in a warm embrace, no words

needed between the two women as protocol was pushed aside to the delight of the room and they hugged each other.

'Your Majesty.' Maria swept in a curtsy with her babe in arms as Alex, the man who would have reluctantly been King, deeply bowed.

'Effie!' Stefania smiled. 'To you I am Effie…'

'Better you than me.' Prince Alex smiled, then kissed his half sister's hand.

And time was of the essence, yet still Effie lingered, tracing her finger along their little baby's cheeks. Little Alexandria—named in honour of her father—was the most beautiful little girl, with her daddy's dark eyes and her mother's gorgeous curls.

Effie had insisted children and babies be allowed—the aides and courtiers had baulked, yet the babies, Effie had insisted, were the most precious jewels, they were the future, and they needed to be seen.

And tonight they were seen.

Prince Andreas and his wife, Holly, both standing with babes in arms, having flown in from Australia to share in this precious day.

'The gorgeous twins…' A delicious little girl named Sophia who went easily from her father's grasp and snuggled into the new Queen's neck as Holly and Effie laughed.

'Nicholas is still a little shy,' Holly explained.

'You will let him get used to us?' Effie checked. Andreas had returned to his love in Australia and had been utterly prepared to denounce everything, if it meant he could be with Holly, yet he had returned for this day.

'Of course.' Holly smiled, feeling the blissful weight of her son in her arms and relishing it, herself no longer scared of her husband's title, just safe with his love. 'You will see us often.'

'From Greece, Princess Katarina of Aristo…' Hassan duly announced, but Effie wasn't listening.

Effie held Kitty in her arms for a moment, then smiled at her half sister, who texted and emailed her often, who told her that she was beautiful and who, out of all of them, was the closest to her heart, because she had battled the same demons as Effie with her self-image, and had won.

'Anastasia is gorgeous!'

Effie's heart split in two as she gazed at Nikos and Kitty's daughter, named after Nikos's dead mother, and the happiness the little family imbued warmed her.

'She is not so beautiful at 3:00 a.m.' Kitty smiled, but there was no more time to chat; already she was being moved on.

'Princess Elissa Karedes…' Hassan said needlessly as Effie greeted her other half sister.

'You look stunning!' Lissa squeezed her hands.

'So do you…' Effie smiled as she took in Lissa's stunning dress. 'Tino Dranias.' Effie checked, sure that stunning designer dress Lissa was wearing was one of his creations, her smile widening as Lissa nodded. 'I am learning.'

'We all are.' Lissa smiled through tears.

'You are happy in Sydney?' Effie asked.

'So happy.' Lissa nodded. 'I see Holly and Andreas a lot.'

Only Hassan was moving her on.

To crowned queens and kings of Europe, to princes from foreign lands, and Zakari should be two steps behind her, Effie thought as she struggled with a nameless face, yet he was held up, was facing a duty that would inflame and irritate at times, only now she understood that duty for the most part prevailed.

The family was a pleasure, but staring down at the row of people yet to meet, Effie felt her stamina falter, Hassan's voice fading in and out. Effie missed the introduction to her next guest, trying frantically to place him, confused, because his black eyes looked familiar somehow, only she couldn't work out the man's name, trying to catch Hassan's attention, but he was speaking into his mouthpiece.

'I hope you have enjoyed the day…' Effie smiled, realising she'd just have to wing it.

'It has been a pleasure, Your Majesty.' He bowed gracefully, and kissed her hand.

The room was so hot, Zakari was just a couple of people behind, and, staring down the line, Effie realised that there were just a few more people to get through.

Only she couldn't.

"Your Majesty?' She could hear the question in the dignitary's voice as she gripped his hand tighter.

'Forgive me,' she gasped. 'I do not feel well, do not let me shame myself…'

'It is okay.' His voice was calm and even and he gripped her hand as the dizziness abated, the appalling wash of nausea settling. 'Just breathe,' he said gently as Effie blew softly out, staring, focussing on the fingers that gripped hers as she dragged in another lungful of air, just determined not to faint.

'I will pretend that you are talking with me,' the dignitary said. 'No one will notice. Just keep taking slow, deep breaths.'

'Thank you.' She could feel the chill of her cold

sweat abate, this unknown man's words coming from not such a distance now. 'Thank you,' Effie said again, clasping his hand in gratitude and staring, frowning at the scars on his wrist…her fuddled mind trying to fathom where she had seen them before…

'Effie?' Zakari's hand was around her waist. "Enough…we will go and get some cool water and then we will bid farewell to everyone. You are exhausted.'

"Thank you.' Effie smiled into the dark eyes of the man who had saved her from shaming herself.

'Come.' Zakari's hand was around her, leading her to seclusion, thrusting icy cool water to her lips and pouring it down her throat. 'Today has been too long.'

'It is fine.'

'You were up before dawn, now it ends. It is too much.'

'It's the coronation. I can't just go home because I am tired.'

'You are unwell…' Fiercely protective, Zakari refused to relent. 'You were as white as a sheet in there. You are clearly exhausted.'

'I'm very well.' Effie smiled. 'Thanks to that lovely man, I was saved from embarrassing myself… Zakari, who was he?' Effie frowned as again she tried to recall. 'Just as I was about to faint I saw there were marks on—'

'You were about to faint!' Zakari was appalled. 'Enough—I will tell Hassan you are unwell, and to prepare the guests for your departure…'

'Zakari, I am not sick…' Effie's smile widened. 'Remember how Kalila was so pale and unwell…' She watched Zakari's face stiffen as realisation hit. 'It is completely normal to feel like this, apparently…'

'A baby?' His voice was hoarse. He had congratulated his brothers, had held nieces and nephews, had assumed he would know how he felt if ever they were graced with the news, but to hear her say it, to hear on her coronation day that Effie was having a baby, their baby, told him all was right in the world.

That all was well on both islands brought a peace to his soul he had never expected.

That there would be a rightful heir made the future never brighter.

But for that moment, none of that mattered.

'If it is a boy we will call him Zafir,' Effie said softly.

'And if it is a girl, she will be Lydia.'

How nice it was to say their names out loud—and smile as they did so.

That all the secrets were safe now, because they were out.

That their love had united the Kingdom of Adamas.

* * * * *

Harlequin Presents® is thrilled to introduce
a sexy new duet,
HOT BED OF SCANDAL, *by Kelly Hunter!*
Read on for a sneak peek of the first book
EXPOSED: MISBEHAVING WITH THE MAGNATE.

'I'M ATTRACTED to you and don't see why I should deny
it. Our kiss in the garden suggests you're not exactly in-
different to me. The solution seems fairly straightforward.'

'You want me to become the comte's convenient
mistress?'

'I'm not a comte,' Luc said. 'All I have is the castle.'

'All right, the billionaire's preferred plaything, then.'

'I'm not a billionaire, either. Yet.' His lazy smile
warned her it was on his to-do list. 'No, I want you to
become my outrageously beautiful, independently
wealthy lover.'

'Isn't that the same option?'

'No, you might have noticed that the wording's a
little different.'

'They're just words, Luc. The outcome's the same.'

'It's an attitude thing.' He looked at her, his smile
crookedly charming. 'So what do you say?'

To an affair with the likes of Luc Duvalier? 'I say it's
dangerous. For both of us.'

Luc's eyes gleamed. 'There is that.'

'Not to mention insane.'

'Quite possibly. Was that a yes?'

Gabrielle really didn't know what to say. 'So how do we start this thing? If I were to agree to it. Which I haven't.' Yet.

'We start with dinner. Tonight. No expectations beyond a pleasant evening with fine food, fine wine and good company. And we see what happens.'

'I don't know,' she said, reaching for her coffee. 'It seems a little…'

'Straightforward?' he suggested. 'Civilized?'

'For us, yes,' she murmured. 'Where would we eat? Somewhere public or in private?'

'Somewhere public,' he said firmly. 'The restaurant I'm thinking of is a fine one—excellent food, small premises and always busy. A man might take his lover there if he was trying to keep his hands off her.'

'Would I meet you there?' she said.

'I will, of course, collect you,' he said, playing the autocrat and playing it well. 'Shall I meet you there,' he murmured in disbelief. 'What kind of question is that?'

'Says the new generation Frenchman,' she countered. 'Liberated, egalitarian, nonsexist…'

'Helpful, attentive, chivalrous…' he added with a reckless smile. 'And very beddable.'

He was that.

'All right,' she said. 'I'll give you the day—and tonight—to prove that a civilized, pleasurable and man-ageable affair wouldn't be beyond us. If you can prove this to my satisfaction, I'll make love with you. If this gets out of hand, however…'

'Yes?' he said silkily. 'What do you suggest?'

Gabrielle leaned forward, elbows on the table. Luc

leaned forward, too. 'Well, I don't know about you,' she murmured, 'but I'm a clever, outrageously beautiful, independently wealthy woman. I plan to run.'

This sparky story is full of passion, wit and scandal and will leave you wanting more!
Look for
EXPOSED: MISBEHAVING WITH THE MAGNATE
Available March 2010

Two families torn apart by secrets and desire
are about to be reunited in

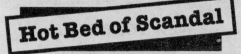

a sexy new duet by

Kelly Hunter

EXPOSED: MISBEHAVING WITH THE MAGNATE

#2905 Available March 2010

Gabriella Alexander returns to the French vineyard she
was banished from after being caught in flagrante with the
owner's son Lucien Duvalier–only to finish what they started!

REVEALED: A PRINCE AND A PREGNANCY

#2913 Available April 2010

Simone Duvalier wants Rafael Alexander and always has, but
they both get more than they bargained for when a night of
passion and a royal revelation rock their world!

BRAVO FAMILY TIES

A BRIDE FOR JERICHO BRAVO

Marnie Jones had long ago buried her wild-child
impulses and opted to be "safe," romantically
speaking. But one look at born rebel Jericho Bravo
and she began to wonder if her thrill-seeking side
was about to be revived. Because if ever there was
a man worth taking a chance on, there he was,
right within her grasp....

*Available in March
wherever books are sold.*

LARGER-PRINT BOOKS!

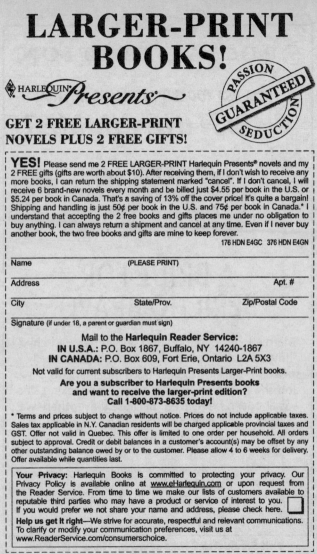

HARLEQUIN *Presents*~

PASSION GUARANTEED SEDUCTION

GET 2 FREE LARGER-PRINT NOVELS PLUS 2 FREE GIFTS!

YES! Please send me 2 FREE LARGER-PRINT Harlequin Presents® novels and my 2 FREE gifts (gifts are worth about $10). After receiving them, if I don't wish to receive any more books, I can return the shipping statement marked "cancel". If I don't cancel, I will receive 6 brand-new novels every month and be billed just $4.55 per book in the U.S. or $5.24 per book in Canada. That's a saving of 13% off the cover price! It's quite a bargain! Shipping and handling is just 50¢ per book in the U.S. and 75¢ per book in Canada.* I understand that accepting the 2 free books and gifts places me under no obligation to buy anything. I can always return a shipment and cancel at any time. Even if I never buy another book, the two free books and gifts are mine to keep forever.

176 HDN E4GC   376 HDN E4GN

Name _____ (PLEASE PRINT)

Address _____ Apt. #

City _____ State/Prov. _____ Zip/Postal Code

Signature (if under 18, a parent or guardian must sign)

Mail to the Harlequin Reader Service:
IN U.S.A.: P.O. Box 1867, Buffalo, NY 14240-1867
IN CANADA: P.O. Box 609, Fort Erie, Ontario L2A 5X3

Not valid for current subscribers to Harlequin Presents Larger-Print books.

**Are you a subscriber to Harlequin Presents books and want to receive the larger-print edition?
Call 1-800-873-8635 today!**

* Terms and prices subject to change without notice. Prices do not include applicable taxes. Sales tax applicable in N.Y. Canadian residents will be charged applicable provincial taxes and GST. Offer not valid in Quebec. This offer is limited to one order per household. All orders subject to approval. Credit or debit balances in a customer's account(s) may be offset by any other outstanding balance owed by or to the customer. Please allow 4 to 6 weeks for delivery. Offer available while quantities last.

Your Privacy: Harlequin Books is committed to protecting your privacy. Our Privacy Policy is available online at www.eHarlequin.com or upon request from the Reader Service. From time to time we make our lists of customers available to reputable third parties who may have a product or service of interest to you. If you would prefer we not share your name and address, please check here. ☐

Help us get it right—We strive for accurate, respectful and relevant communications. To clarify or modify your communication preferences, visit us at www.ReaderService.com/consumerschoice.

HPLP10

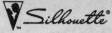

ROMANTIC
SUSPENSE

Sparked by Danger, Fueled by Passion.

Introducing a brand-new miniseries
Lawmen of Black Rock

Peyton Wilkerson's life shatters when her
four-month-old daughter, Lilly, vanishes.
But handsome sheriff Tom Grayson is
determined to put the pieces together and
reunite her with her baby. Will Tom be able
to protect Peyton and Lilly while fighting
his own growing feelings?

Find out in
His Case, Her Baby
by
CARLA CASSIDY

Available in March wherever books are sold

HARLEQUIN *Presents*

Coming Next Month
Available February 23, 2010